T0148055

Connect All the Missing Pieces of Your Life

Regina E. Rosier

iUniverse, Inc.
New York   Bloomington

Connect All the Missing Pieces of Your Life

This is a work of fiction. All of the characters, names, incidents, organizations, and dialogue in this novel are either the products of the author's imagination or are used fictitiously.

iUniverse books may be ordered through booksellers or by contacting:

iUniverse
1663 Liberty Drive
Bloomington, IN 47403
www.iuniverse.com
1-800-Authors (1-800-288-4677)

ISBN: 978-1-4502-0656-3 (sc)
ISBN: 978-1-4502-0655-6 (ebk)

Printed in the United States of America

iUniverse rev. date: 3/12/2010

To my son Andre,
Thanks for always being there.
Love you forever!
Mom

Also by Regina E. Rosier
The Depth of My Darkness, The Radiance of My Essence

Connect all the Missing Pieces of your Life

I stepped out of the shower on a hot June summer morning in Brooklyn's Red Hook Projects. As I stood on the bare, cold bathroom floor, the loud ringing of the wall phone in my kitchen startled me. I hastily walked to the kitchen and grabbed the phone. I held it with my left hand and tried to hold the towel with my right hand. Water dripped down my legs and splashed around my feet. I had just turned sixteen and was preparing for work at my first job.

"Hello?" I said.

"Hi, I need to speak with Bailey Branch."

I did not recognize this woman's voice.

"This is Bailey Branch. Who is this?"

"I'm Martha Nance, one of the nurses from the downtown Belle-Brooklyn Sanatorium. I was told to call you about your mother, Paisley Branch. The reason why I'm calling is to let you know that your mother died this morning."

"What? Mom died?"

I wanted to hang up, but something told me to hear her out.

I started to feel faint. My legs felt wobbly. Slowly I leaned against one of the kitchen counters to compose myself. I held the phone so close to my ear that I'm sure it left a dent.

"What happened? Mom was fine when I visited with her a couple of days ago."

"I'm not at liberty to discuss that with you. I'm only the messenger. You have to talk to her doctor about that," she said matter of factly.

"You mean Dr. Baxter? I want to speak with him right away."

"You can't. He left an hour ago for a two-day conference."

I felt frustrated. None of this was making sense to me.

"Her body is in our temporary morgue. You need to come for her belongings as soon as possible. Otherwise they will be discarded. I'll box them up and have them ready for you."

"Nurse–" A harsh dial tone sounded. What kind of place is this that would deliver devastating news over the phone like that? Isn't that unethical? I may be young but I know that this doesn't sound right.

After I finished toweling off, I sat down in a deep fog. Mom's gone and I am all alone. She's the only person I've ever loved and now she's gone. And she was the only one in my life who ever showed me any love in this selfish world. I am in deep shock and I feel guilty because I can't even shed a tear.

I feel enraged. I didn't understand how mom allowed herself to slip into a condition that caused her to have to live in an asylum.

We were living a pretty decent life in our quaint little apartment in the late 1960's. I liked our large neighborhood because it was located near the Red Hook Recreational Area. Also the Buttermilk Channel and the Upper New York Bay were nearby. On occasion I could feel the breeze from the Bay. And our neighborhood wasn't too far from the humongous Brooklyn Bridge.

About a month ago out of the blue, everything just went haywire. Mom totally lost it. She tried to jump off of the roof at her job and incredibly the police negotiator was able to talk her down and subdue her. I guess working hard and raising a kid alone stressed her out more than I thought. I'm sure it was difficult for mom to talk to me about things that bothered her but I assumed that since she had what I thought was a girlfriend that she would have confided in her. I obviously was wrong because that girlfriend disappeared soon after mom was admitted into the asylum. I guess she kept most things to herself.

How could a person just give up on everything and everyone and simply slip over the edge? How could a woman who was physically healthy one week be dead the next? I needed an answer. I hung the towel up in the bathroom, went to my room and got dressed, and called Pathmark on Clinton Street where I had just landed a job as a cashier then headed down to the Belle-Brooklyn Sanatorium. I walked through the projects to get to the Smith-9th Streets subway station where I hopped on the F train.

I impatiently sat in my seat observing the loud couple seated across from me. I didn't care to hear their conversation. Why couldn't they sit quietly like the others? The train passed Carroll Street, Bergen Street, and the rest was a blur until I reached my stop at Lexington Ave/63rd Street.

Mom - Paisley Branch

After exiting the train station, I walked several blocks until I reached the sanatorium. At the gate of the dark brick, dingy building it seemed to take forever for someone to buzz me in. When I got inside, the person who buzzed me in was not at the information desk. I paced the hallway until I saw an old, skinny black janitor.

He stopped pushing his broom and said, "Hey Miss, all the doctors are in a meeting right now. So you might be waiting here for a good while."

"Do you know how long this meeting is supposed to last?"

"It's supposed to be about a half hour I think. But they never leave their meetings right away," he said and went back to sweeping the hallway.

It was about one in the afternoon when I sat down and waited to speak with a doctor.

While I sat waiting, I couldn't help but think that mom had been so young and so full of life. If she hadn't been so consumed with working and taking care of me, maybe she would have taken better care of her mental health. Regular visits to the doctor would have probably revealed that all was not well with her and the doctor could have recommended that she see a psychiatrist so that things would not have gotten this far out of control.

After twenty minutes, one of the doctors' receptionists, a young, short, knock-kneed Caucasian woman, came out of one of the offices and walked over to me.

"Bailey?" she asked.

"Yes," I said.

"Follow me," she said as she escorted me into Dr. Matthew's office.

I towered over her. I am 5'7" and weigh one hundred five pounds. I have light milk chocolate skin, round brown eyes and long wavy brown hair. I look a lot like my mom.

"This is Dr. Matthews. Have a seat over there by his desk," she said as she walked out of the room.

Dr. Matthews, a short Caucasian man, looked to be in his middle forties. He had small, beady green eyes that he frequently rubbed. He stood to shake my hand. Then he sat back down, tapped his pen on the desk repeatedly and stared at me all of which got on my nerves.

"Dr. Matthews," I said, "what happened? Mom seemed to be doing fine when I visited her here last weekend."

He ran his fingers through his brown hair.

"At this point," he said, "I have no idea. Ms. Branch, as you probably know, we have a very good program here for people who have your mom's kind of psychological disorder."

"Yes, I know but I never knew the exact details of mom's treatments or what even caused her to lose touch with reality. Dr. Baxter told me mom had to take a number of medications to help her mind function better. But that's all he told me."

The doctor opened a drawer and took out a folder. He looked through some papers in the folder, put his glasses on and said, "Let me see. Your mother was diagnosed with a disorder called Absent Grief. This means she was a survivor of something tragic and was never really able to let go of the overwhelming emotions and circumstances surrounding the tragedy. During one of her many sessions, she told us about some hardships she experienced. I am not sure if you were aware, but some went as far back as her childhood."

"What did she tell you? Did she tell you about what happened to her parents?"

He shifted some papers and said, "Yes, her file indicates that she told us she became an orphan because her parents died in a fire when she was twelve years old. And she never forgave herself for killing them."

"But she didn't kill them. Is that what she told you?"

"We know she didn't kill them, and we tried to work with her to help her resolve this feeling. Let me look here in her file. During one of her sessions she said and I quote, 'It was my parents' anniversary and I surprised them by cooking a big dinner. I wasn't used to cooking but because I had learned how to cook in home economics I figured I'd give it a try. My parents ate their meal in their bedroom and when they were finished they didn't bother taking their plates to the kitchen, which was usually the norm. Anyway, since I snacked while I cooked, I wasn't hungry. So I went to my bedroom, where I fell asleep almost immediately.'

'What seemed like hours later, I was awakened by the sound of someone yelling my name and banging on my bedroom window. Although groggy, I sat up and immediately smelled smoke. I looked around and saw a bright orange light under my bedroom door. I ran over to see if I could open the door but it was too hot. While I screamed for my parents, one of my neighbors had managed to break my window, pull me out and carry me out to safety.'

'I continued crying and yelling for someone to save my parents, but the fire department arrived too late. The house was completely engulfed in flames. It was impossible for anyone to get to my parents, not only because of the flames, but because their room was on the second floor of our two-story house. Hours later after the dust had settled, the fire marshal's preliminary investigation revealed that I had accidentally left the frying pan on a stove burner that I forgot to turn off and this caused the fire.'

'There weren't smoke detectors back then so since my parents were asleep, they had no way of knowing there was a fire. Their room was upstairs at the opposite end of the kitchen. They died of smoke inhalation before the fire even reached them.'

'I was fortunate that one of the neighbors had just arrived home from work and saw the flames shooting out from the kitchen window. He called the fire department then ran over to help. I blamed myself for that fire and never forgot about it. I hated myself for what I did.' End quote."

"She carried that guilt around with her all her life. Since she lived in several different foster homes, she never had the chance to get the counseling she needed. Apparently no one cared enough to ask her how she felt about the whole incident and about the fact that she was now alone without any relatives. Her parents didn't have any siblings so she had no one to turn to. And her grandparents were long gone."

"Sometimes carrying guilt around like that for a long period of time can really drive a person over the brink, especially if that person doesn't seek help to deal with it. In her case, she let this and other stresses in life eventually get the best of her. And she just lost it one day. And that's really sad. It's a doggone shame that no one knew what she was dealing with all of those years. We conducted many sessions with her and prescribed various types and doses of medications which seemed to be working." He then paused for a moment as if he wanted to say something else.

"Dr. Matthews, where's my mom? I want to see her."

"I'm sorry, you can't see her body right now."

"Why not?"

His demeanor gave me the impression that he was trying to be evasive about something.

The phone buzzed and he turned to answer it.

"Jessie, I told you to hold all my calls."

I could tell by the look on his face that the conversation on the phone was really involved.

He stood up and excused himself.

"I'll be right back. Just sit tight."

I sat there for about five minutes wondering what that conversation could have been about. When Dr. Matthews returned, his face was flushed. He seemed upset about something.

"Ms. Branch, I was just informed about something that I didn't know earlier."

He sat down and started shuffling through some papers on his desk.

I started getting impatient.

"What is it?"

"I hate to have to be the one to tell you this, but I was just informed that your mother's body was cremated and um...all her belongings were incinerated."

"Cremated? What are you talking about? She was not supposed to be cremated! There must be some mistake. You must be talking about someone else's mom!"

He lifted his head and looked me squarely in the face.

"No, Ms. Branch. I wish I could say that this was a mistake. But unfortunately the director cremated the body about a half hour ago. I'm really sorry."

"You're sorry? That's all that you can say? What kind of place is this? You people are just as mental as the patients who stay here!"

I stood up and leaned over the desk, clinched my teeth and said, "Where do you people get the nerve to do something as horrible as that? How could you? She might not have meant anything to you all, but she was my mom! She was my blood!" I screamed.

Dr. Matthews stood up and put his hands out.

"Shush, please keep it down. The staff here at Belle-Brooklyn is really sorry for this terrible mistake. And we were assured that this will never happen again."

"I can't believe what I'm hearing. My gut feeling tells me that this is not the first incident of this kind nor will it be the last. How can you doctors expect to find out what caused her death if you didn't keep her body around long enough to at least perform an autopsy? You cremated my mom so quickly. I didn't even have a chance to say good-bye. Don't you have a heart? What kind of idiot is running this place? What are you doctors trying to hide? You discarded my mom as if she was trash! How dare you? She was a loving human being who had rights!"

I was so fired up that I wished I could leap across Dr. Matthews' desk and grab him. He must have read my mind because he pressed a button that sounded a screeching alarm. Within seconds hefty security guards surrounded and tackled me. It wasn't hard because I was a lightweight. I kicked and screamed as they manhandled and carried me out passed the gates. After I was thrown out into the streets, the gate closed firmly behind me.

I am dazed, a little bruised and confused. None of this is making any sense.

After the gate closed, I felt totally shut out. I had been thrown out into the streets like trash.

They threw my mom away. Tears started trickling down my cheeks. After a few minutes I got up, brushed myself off, and left before anyone else had a chance to come after me.

I feel very disheartened because I didn't have any physical things to remember mom by. Well now that I think about it I did have some at home, but the sentimental things were with her and the asylum had incinerated them. I only had them there in hopes of jarring her out of her depression.

It was so depressing to know that mom had died in an asylum alone. She had been all alone with no one there to help her. No one cared but me and a lot of good that did. I feel guilty because I hadn't been there for her. I had let mom down. In her time of need, I let her down. What kind of daughter was I?

I suddenly became angry at the father I never knew. If he hadn't abandoned mom when she was pregnant with me, maybe our life would have gone in a different direction. Maybe he would have been able to help her deal with her tragic past.

Who am I kidding? It probably was for the best anyway. Chances are he would have deserted us later in life, which would have been even more painful. Oh God, wherever you are, I need you. I feel left out in the cold. I don't have any parents, brothers or sisters or any relatives. But I still have you God, don't I?

I can't help wondering what had happened to cause mom's death. I think this place is covering up something.

Best Friends Forever - Bailey and Kahadeja

Thirteen years later…I am alive and well. I survived living conditions in several foster homes and ended up married and pregnant at the age of 17.

"Baby Love, my Baby Love, I need you, oh how I need you…"

The Supremes, gotta love them!

It's a sweltering, muggy afternoon in the projects in Red Hook, Brooklyn during the summer of 1979 as the music from my radio reverberated through the apartment walls and out the windows. The three buildings on my block all had six floors, and the buildings together stood in an L shape.

My twelve-year-old son, Brian, my one-year-old daughter, Bae George, and I lived on the fifth floor of the 749 Henry Street building. The whole neighborhood seemed to be in good spirits. Little girls were outside playing hopscotch, while others were jumping double dutch. I used to love jumping double dutch when I was younger. From time to time, I still manage to jump in during someone's turn. The girls just love it when I go out of my way to play with them.

Some boys were on the pavement playing tops while others were busy in the streets, running through the water that spewed out from the fire hydrant.

Brian, who is a scrawny brown skinned boy, was with them trying his hardest to keep up with the older boys. He had always seemed so precocious for his age. His father died when he was young so he never really had a father figure in his life. And I never took the time to date so that he could have a man in his life so because of this Brian looked up to the older boys in our community. My biggest fear was losing him to the wrong crowd. So I consciously found myself always keeping a close eye on his activities.

Despite my loud music, I managed to hear the phone ring. It was my best friend and neighbor Kahadeja Cummings, a beautiful caramel-colored young lady in her late twenties with long ebony hair that cascaded in braids down to her shoulders. She's a curvaceous 5'7" one hundred fifty pound young woman who has piercing brown eyes that she over accentuates by drawing black liner over her eyebrows. She too is a single parent of a scrawny twelve-year-old boy, Miles. He has skin the color of chestnut and is slightly taller than Brian. Miles was the result of a two-year passionate love affair with a married friend.

"What's up?" I said when I picked up the phone.

"Girl! You gotta look out the window!"

"Why?"

"It's Carla and Norma! They're fighting again over Carla's no good husband!"

I hung up the phone, ran over to the window, and saw that neighbors were hanging out of windows watching too.

Carla was about 5'11" and had big breasts, thick ashy legs and arms, and hips so wide that it would take two chairs to seat her! She had big gray wide-set eyes, blotchy chocolate-colored skin, and short auburn cornrows braided back away from her face. She was wearing a matching red shorts set and a pair of big brown sandals.

Norma, who was about the same height, had beady brown eyes, cocoa-colored skin, and her hair was fixed in two short Afro puffs, one on each side of her head, covered by a black band around her head. She basically had the same kind of physique. She thought she was cute in her yellow halter-top with a matching yellow flair skirt. As big as she was, she shouldn't have been wearing this kind of outfit with her flab hanging out everywhere. But this didn't phase her one bit. In her mind, she was fine and that was all that mattered.

Fighting seemed to be their summer ritual. To make matters worse, both women lived in the same building! Even though Larry was living with Carla, he seemed to think he was God's gift to women. He had two kids with Carla, and one with Norma, all close in age. He always went back and forth between the two, and these women were stupid enough to play his game and take him back. They were so busy trying to prove something to the other that they were blinded as to how ridiculous they looked.

If you saw Larry, you would have thought that both of these women should have been put away. He was short, skinny and looked like a black weasel. He was such a sleaze. On any given day, when he stepped out to hang with his boys, he'd be wearing his favorite tight black faux leather pants, a short-collared black shirt, heavy gold chains, and his worn-out banana-yellow platform shoes. He almost always dressed that hot in the summertime! What a sight! Yuck!

Carla and Norma were screaming obscenities while tugging and pulling on each other's hair and clothes. Their filthy, snotty-nosed children were standing around crying. Larry was sitting on a bench drinking a can of Colt 45 beer laughing with his friends. He finally stood up to break up the fight after the women started tearing off each other's clothes. There was blood, hair and pieces of clothing everywhere. Larry pulled Carla off Norma and while he was doing this, Norma managed to get in another couple of sucker punches to Carla's nose. She tried her hardest to break it. One of the bystanders restrained Norma.

Carla put up her fists and exclaimed, "You…you better stay away from my man and get some business of your own, he's mine!"

Norma put her hands on her big hips, wiggled her neck, and yelled, "I do have some business of my own, and don't tell me what to do. I can have your man anytime I want. He's my baby's daddy, and you better not ever forget that!"

Carla turned around and started hitting on Larry.

"You jerk, you should have never gotten involved with that cheap chick! How could you do this to me and the kids?"

Carla snatched her kids and started walking into their apartment building.

Norma slid her large hands down her body and taunted, "That's right, you better go! You chicken! You can't even fight right. As a matter of fact, you can't do a lot of things right. That's why Larry keeps coming back to me! I know how to take care of his needs!"

Carla ignored her and kept on walking.

Larry walked over to Norma and said, "Ah, shut up and give it a rest. Go upstairs and clean yourself off. You disgust me."

Norma spat in his face and quickly went into the building. Larry wiped his face with the back of his left hand and stood there looking like a fool in front of his friends and in front of all of the neighborhood spectators. He turned around and went upstairs…

Kahadeja, or Deja as everybody calls her, stopped by after the melee. As she sat down on my couch, she said, "Girl, when are those two gonna give up that no good dude?"

I sat down next to her after I turned down my music.

"I don't know but I hope for the kids' sake that it'll be real soon. It's so embarrassing to have all of your business out in the streets like that."

"But you know how those two are," Deja said, "they are so ghetto anyway. Can you imagine sharing a guy while the whole neighborhood knows about it? And could you imagine the germs that are being spread? Ugh!"

"Yeah, the sad part about it is most of the time history repeats itself. And with parents like those, these kids don't have a fighting chance."

A knock on the door broke up the conversation.

"Oh girl," I said, "I forgot that I'm supposed to do Janice's hair."

I walked over to the door and opened it and said, "Come in Janice and sit down on that chair in the kitchen."

"Ok, oh hi Deja," Janice said as she walked in.

"Hi girl," Deja said.

Janice is an athletic 5'8" one hundred fifty five pound young woman who has cocoa brown skin. She's all muscle. She's in her late twenties and single but unlike us she has no children. Most people like her not only because of her athleticism but also because she has a trustworthy spirit and a trusting smile.

I stood behind Janice and started combing through her bushy short honey brown hair.

"I already washed and blow dried it," Janice said.

"Janice, you didn't wash it with Prell shampoo again, did you? You know that shampoo is not made for black people's hair!"

"No, Bailey, I now only use Afro Sheen products."

"Ok then, let's get started."

I turned on one of the burners and took my straightening comb out of the drawer. While the straightening comb was heating up on the front burner, I greased a small section of Janice's hair with green Bergamot grease.

"Ok, now hold still," I said as I wiped the comb on a paper towel to test it, because if that burned I knew it would burn her hair. It didn't burn the paper towel so I straightened all of her hair, and then it was time to do the back of her head and the edges.

"Bay, how did you learn how to straighten hair? With the kind of hair you have, we know you never had to straighten your own." Deja stated.

Janice tried to look up at Kahadeja.

"Hush Deja, let her concentrate. I don't want her to burn me."

"Don't worry, I'm not gonna burn your naps," I said.

"Hey, I felt that heat," Janice said.

"Janice, we go through this every time. If you don't hold still, I won't be able to straighten your edges and you'll walk right out of here with straight hair and nappy edges!"

Janice decided to shut up after that.

"In answer to your question Deja, my mom was black and she had thick coarse hair. I used to sit and watch her every move when she straightened her hair and some of my girlfriends' hair. They used to get annoyed at me because I didn't have to go through that process like they did. I couldn't help it that my long wavy hair wasn't kinky enough for a straightening comb."

After I straightened Janice's hair, I used a small-barreled hot curling iron to curl all of her hair, section by section up to her scalp. I left it that way so that she could style it the way that she wanted to later. It turned out good and she was pleased when she looked at it in the bathroom mirror.

"Thank you Bailey. Here you go." She handed me some cash because she appreciated my convenient services plus she knew that straightening her hair had my apartment smelling like burnt hair, which was a smell that I hated.

"I'll see you back in this chair next week. And try not to sweat your hair out with all your wild dancing tonight."

"Bailey please," Janice said as she headed towards the door.

"Girl you know that once you get on the dance floor and start feeling the groove, you can't sit down. You gotta dance to every record that plays."

"I can't help it if I love to dance! I can't sit around like you two looking pretty and gossiping about everyone!" Janice said with a smile as she paused at the door.

Deja got up and said, "Well Bay she's right about that. But Janice baby don't knock it until you try it honey. I gotta go and get ready for tonight. See you two there." She kissed me on the cheek and left.

"All right, see you two later."

There was going to be a party at Deja's place that night and she wanted everything to be just right. She planned this party a month ago.

It was starting to get dark, and I needed to send Brian to the store before dinner. I went to the window and yelled for him. It's amazing how your kid can be down the block or around the corner and still manage to hear you when he's called.

When Brian appeared I called down to him and said, "I need you to go to Pablo's to get some sugar for the Kool-Aid."

I had the change already wrapped up in a handkerchief and dropped it down to him.

"And make sure you come right back!"

About twenty minutes later, Brian busted into the apartment with sugar in one hand and change in the other.

"Here you go mom," he said breathlessly as he put the sugar on the kitchen counter.

"Thanks baby. Go wash your hands and come set the table. Dinner's almost ready. And make sure you do this quietly. Bae George just went to sleep."

After Brian washed his hands, we sat down at our small table and talked about the day while we ate our dinner.

"Mom, I'm tired of eating chopped up spaghetti. Why can't we eat ribs or chops like Miles?"

"Baby, one day we will, but we can't right now."

"But why not?"

"Because I can't afford to buy that right now. It's not in the budget. Deja is fortunate enough to get money from Miles' dad, so she can afford to buy all the chops and ribs she wants. You probably don't remember, but we used to eat all of that stuff when your dad was alive. This is only temporary because we'll eat stuff like that again, but until then, be glad you have something to eat. I chopped it up to make more to last until tomorrow."

"Mom—"

"Brian, this part of the conversation is over. You hear me? Now eat your spaghetti. I'm sure some of the children around here would be more than happy to have your portion."

"Ok mom, you're right. Sorry I didn't mean to sound so unappreciative." He leaned across the table and kissed me.

"I know you're taking care of me and Bae George by yourself and I thank you for it. I love you mom."

"I love you too, Brian."

I tried to make sure that these important 'I Love You' words were spoken between us on a regular basis. Brian and Bae George are the loves of my life. I love them with every inch of my heart. Brian has been growing up so nicely. I am so proud of him. I pondered that while I ate my dinner.

"Brian, I'm so proud of you," I said.

"Thanks mom, but where'd that come from?" Brian asked.

"Don't worry about it. You know how moms can be."

"Yeah, you're right. Moms can be so confusing. Oh well, can you please pass the ketchup?"

"Ketchup? Oh no, don't tell me that you're gonna drown my spaghetti again?"

"You know it! Can you pass the Kool-Aid pitcher too?"

"Sure baby."

After dinner I went into the bedroom and checked up on Bae George and found that she was still knocked out cold. So Brian and I sat on the couch in the living room.

"Brian, Miles is coming over here tonight."

"Great, but why?"

"Because Deja is having the party of the summer, and both of you will be baby-sitting your sister. You can stay up and watch TV but just make sure that you check in on her from time to time. She's down for the night, and I already filled a bottle with formula. All you have to do is make sure that you put a little bit of cereal in it. Be careful if you have to heat one up, and make sure you remember to turn the stove off. She's really getting too old for a bottle now, so I just want you to use it if all else fails. You know what to do. And Deja's apartment is only a few steps away, so if there is an emergency just have Miles run out to get one of us. You're dependable so I know that everything will be all right."

Miles arrived around 8:50 p.m. carrying a brown paper bag under his arm.

"Hi Miss Branch."

"Hello Miles, come in and make yourself at home."

"Ok," he said as he walked passed me into the living room.

"Hi Brian. Here, mom bought some snacks for us."

"Cool," Brian said as he started pulling things out of the bag.

I was getting ready to leave so I kissed Brian on the temple and whispered, "Love you." I didn't want to embarrass him in front of his friend. Brian looked up at me and smiled.

"Ok," I said, "I checked everything out, the stove's off, my iron is off, so you all should be okay. I suppose you could have done it but anyway I already popped Jiffy Pop popcorn for you two. It's in a bowl on the kitchen counter. Miles thanks for coming over and keeping Brian company. I really appreciate it."

It was 9 o'clock that evening when I walked over to Deja's place. I'm sure that everyone could hear the music blocks away. I walked into her dimly lit apartment and stood for a minute while my eyes adjusted to the surroundings.

Deja liked everything dark. That way she could display her black light posters, with her favorite red light bulb. The posters displayed a man and a woman with big Afros posing in some very suggestive positions. At least two of the posters had nude men and women on them. Deja called this art, but I wasn't into this kind of art and wasn't particularly enthused about letting Brian see these posters, at least not at his age, so I usually made sure that I didn't have a reason to send him over there. Besides, Miles spent a lot of time at our place anyway. Since he and Brian were in the same grade they always worked together on their homework and on projects at my place.

I looked carefully through the crowd and found Deja standing at her small makeshift bar.

"Hey girl, I like your outfit!" Deja shouted as she swayed to the music.

"Thanks Deja."

I had on a red and white mini-dress, and my favorite red go-go boots my husband George had bought me years earlier for an anniversary. I was totally surprised because at the time I knew we were struggling to make ends meet. He was cognizant of the fact that red was my favorite color, and when I saw these boots at Abraham & Strauss I just fell in love with them.

George was with me that day when I tried them on. He must have seen the expression on my face after I tried them on. We couldn't afford them but I wanted to see how I looked in them anyway.

After we left Abraham & Strauss I put the boots out of my mind. It was sweet of George to later buy them for me. I treasured these boots and the love that went along with them. While I was thinking about the past, Deja nudged me and pulled me out of my reverie.

Deja was always a little different. She was ostentatious and gregarious and always stood out in a crowd. She was usually the life of the party and knew that all eyes were focused on her. And why not? She's good looking and has a great outgoing personality. People are naturally drawn to her.

Deja wore spiked pale-green sequined pumps and had on a pale-green bubble dress, a style that was popular in the fifties. This was a cute dress with a bubblelike skirt and a fitted bodice. This dress definitely made her stand out.

"Deja, this dress is so cute girl!"

"Bay, I'm glad you like it." She twirled around to show it off.

"This is my mom's. She takes good care of all of her old things. And doesn't mind if I borrow something from time to time as long as I return it in good condition."

"Gee what a mom."

I'm glad Deja's mom is alive and well. I never want her to experience the deep pain and empty void that I've felt everyday since mom died.

I requested a screwdriver drink from her friend Barney the bartender and walked over and sat down on Deja's couch. I was watching the other guests dance when someone, who was louder than the music, walked in the door. By this time, Deja had put on more lights so that people could see where they were dancing. Of course Janice was one of them. She looked cute in her short one-piece blue linen dress and chic white low-heeled espadrilles. This dress accentuated her nice athletic build. She was having fun grooving to the music.

When I looked over to the door, I had to put my hand up to my mouth.

"Oh, my God! Uh-oh! I gotta get up and grab Deja," I muttered under my breath.

At that same moment Deja's eyes found mine. She was still over at the bar so she traipsed over and tried to sit down next to me on her bright pink leather couch. Her bubble dress made it a little difficult but somehow she managed.

"What's she doing here? She wasn't invited!" Deja said.

"Never mind that girl, what ya gonna do about it?" I asked knowing that although I'm not into fighting I don't have a problem watching a fight.

Deja said, "Shucks, I'm not gonna do anything. Norma's much bigger than I am and she can kick my butt up and down the block. I'm not foolish enough to mess with her."

"Me either."

We sat and watched as Norma walked in carrying a bottle of cheap Vodka while her entourage, which included Larry, lagged behind her. Carla must have been babysitting again. Larry was a bully who used manipulation to force his wife, Carla, to conveniently do things for him that she ordinarily wouldn't do. In this instance, it's babysitting Norma's kid. He reasons that after all it's half his kid too, and if she wants to be with him, she has to do what he says. Isn't that something? He refers to his other kid as *it*. Carla never won the arguments, so depending on whether she felt like fighting or not, she usually ended up giving in to him. She put up with his crap just so she could say that she has a man. That's stupid.

The music was thumping. Since we were mainly into the older artists, the D.J. played music by artists such as Marvin Gaye and Tammi Terrell, The Four Tops, The Chi-Lites, The Temptations as well as a host of many others. He played my favorite song by Marvin and

Tammi which is *You're All I Need to Get By*. The part where Marvin or Tammi sings 'And when I lose my will. You'll be there to push me up the hill' makes it such an emotional song for me. I always thought that George would be there to push me up the hill whenever I started feeling like life was dragging me down. I guess that part of the song now has to apply to Deja. She's always been there. I know that she'll be there to push me up the hill when and if the time ever comes.

No one had the nerve to say anything to Norma so they let her be and hoped her visit would be short lived. Boy, were we glad when she left the party about an hour later.

You would have thought that she wouldn't have wanted anybody to see the scratches on her face from that fight. From what we heard, she broke Carla's nose, which caused her to have two black eyes. Imagine the pain! That Larry is such a jive turkey for stepping out with Norma after all that ruckus.

The party was a success as always. That's Deja, the party animal. She knows how to throw a party! She saw to it that no one got sloppy drunk and thank goodness there weren't any fights. Surprisingly, the old ladies on our floor didn't call the cops on us. They usually called the cops if they heard any noise above a whisper! Back in their day, they were probably bigger party animals than we are!

I had fun doing the bump with one of our friends, Paul. Deja couldn't do the bump because of her bubble dress. But that didn't stop her from doing all of the other dances like the robot and the hustle. When Marvin Gaye's song *Let's Get It On* started playing she even tried to slow dance in that dress. Silly girl!

The party was over around 2 a.m. the next morning.

"Come on Bay. Get off the couch. Let's go over to your place and finish off the rest of these hors d'oeuvres and chicken wings. Boy, what a combination. Anyway I'll clean up later," Deja said as she stood up and picked up the tray.

"Deja, I'll grab the wine. There's only a little bit left. Waste not want not. Isn't that the saying? Or am I off? Anyway, who cares, come on," I said.

We checked on the kids. All was sound. The boys had fallen asleep on the couch with the television blaring. I turned off the television and put a blanket on the floor and moved the boys onto the blanket. Neither one of them even stirred. Bae George too was sound asleep.

"Deja, do you know what time it is?"

"Yep! It's gossip time."

"True that. Come on, let's go to my room. Bring the hors d'oeuvres and wings. I got the wine, and the wine glasses."

We sat up for hours, munching and gossiping about any and everybody. That was our usual way of unwinding after one of Deja's mega parties.

Bailey and George

That summer went by quickly. There were more parties and more fights. There was even a citywide blackout but fortunately all were accounted for and were safe. That night was very stressful for me. As usual Brian was outside somewhere playing with Miles and with some other boys. Sometimes they go around the corner or down the street to Pablo's store without my knowledge. So when the blackout happened, I was a nervous wreck. I was drinking a Coke and Deja was drinking a beer while we sat curled up on my couch fully absorbed watching *Psycho*.

"Oh no, they were about to get to the good part!" I exclaimed.

Deja stood up and walked over to the window.

"Ah Bay. It looks like all of the lights are out in the projects. Do you have a flashlight? We need to go look for the boys," Deja said in a calm tone.

"Oh my goodness! What if something happened to Brian? I would just die!"

Deja found me in the darkness and held my shoulders and said, "Bay, keep it together, we don't have a lot of time. Where is your flashlight?"

"Um, I think it's under my bed," I said as I tried to feel my way into my bedroom.

I came out with it on and saw Deja holding Bae George.

"Come on."

We made our way down the stairs and saw people looking for their kids too. We also saw people running around with what looked like goods. We figured that they must have been stolen because it was unusual to see people running around with televisions, boxed stereo sound systems and mounds of clothes still on hangers. Others were carrying groceries. I saw people carrying a lot of meat and alcohol. That was odd. How do you steal in the dark? Why would you steal? It made no sense to me.

We walked in the direction of Pablo's all the while calling out for the boys. We finally found them the nearest block over from the store, hunched down at someone's entryway.

They ran over to us. Brian spoke first.

"Mom, we figured that since we couldn't see, we would try to feel our way along the building and get to a stopping point, figuring that you would find us."

"That was okay, right mom?" Miles added.

"Yes Miles. We're glad to see that you two stuck together and used your brains and are all right. Come on, let's go," Deja said as we walked back safely to the apartment.

We later found out that there was a lot of looting and other crimes in the city that night. I am so glad that we weren't out in the middle of it. We might have been if it wasn't for the fact that we just had to stay home to watch *Psycho*.

About a month later, it was time to get Brian ready for school. It's times like this when I really miss my husband, George. He died less than two years ago.

I still vividly remember the events surrounding that painful time in our lives. George was 6'2" and was normally a healthy strapping man. He fell ill but kept shrugging it off as a bad cold or the flu. We were sitting around on that October evening watching the sitcom *Good Times* when George started coughing uncontrollably. I thought he was going to choke to death. I had an uneasy feeling about this illness.

"George," I said, "you need to take some time off from work to go to the doctor."

"Bailey, I don't need to go to the doctor. It's probably just the flu."

"Then why are you also having chest pains sometimes? And you have been having an unusual amount of headaches lately and you're restless and you're always going back and forth to the bathroom."

"Bailey, you worry too much," George said in a dismissive tone.

I was so agitated because he refused to go to the doctor. He was so adamant about it so I finally gave up trying. I did everything I could think of to help him get rid of the flu. When he had a fever I rubbed him down with rubbing alcohol. At night I rubbed Vicks on his chest, gave him Tylenol, plenty of liquids, and kept a close eye on his temperature. I was even afraid that he might have a heart attack because of the increase in chest pains. But sadly, all of this was to no avail.

I remember that fateful day when I received a call from one of the nurses at Long Island Hospital. She appeared to have a cold, uncaring attitude, with no compassion at all.

"Is this Mrs. Johnson?" she asked.

"Yes, it is, who is this?"

"This is Helen Wright, I'm a nurse at the Long Island Hospital's emergency room. You need to get here quickly. It's about your husband."

"What? My husband's at work."

"No he's not. He's here."

"Is he all right?"

"You need to get here quickly."

I sat there listening to the dial tone for I don't know how long. I was totally in shock. Ten-year-old Brian was at a friend's so I called over there and told him to stay until I got back. After hanging up the phone, I ran to the train station and hopped on one of the express trains.

It seemed to take forever for the train to arrive at my destination. By then I was a nervous wreck. I ran down two city blocks and into the emergency room, requesting nurse Wright. Someone pointed her out and said, "She's over there."

I walked over to a paunchy black nurse, who I could tell was wearing a curly, short brunette wig. My voice was quivering as I said, "Excuse me, nurse Wright."

She turned around to face me with her clipboard in her hands and said, "Yes?"

"I'm Mrs. Johnson. You called me about my husband, George Johnson."

"I don't recall. The woman who I spoke with was a black woman. I assume that you must be a relative or a girlfriend?"

"What? Girlfriend, no, I'm his wife!"

She looked me up and down, and right when I was about to demand to speak to a supervisor, she said, "Sorry, I just figured that Mrs. Johnson was a black woman. You look so so—"

"Don't hold back now sister, spare me. You mean I look so white!" I interjected.

I started to get loud, and she noticed how annoyed I was becoming so she pointed me in the direction of George's room. I get a lot of these ridiculous reactions because I am light milk chocolate with freckles, due in part to my parents' interracial relationship. To make matters worse, my hair cascades down my back. I normally keep it up in a bun, but I didn't have time today due to the circumstances.

I knocked on the door of emergency room 202 and walked in.

"George?" I said.

The room had one bed that was near the window. The curtains were drab and the room smelled like sickness. Just like a hospital I thought to myself.

I saw a lot of doctors and nurses standing around the bed, which made it difficult for me to see George.

"What's going on?" I inquired.

When they turned around, I saw that a white sheet covered up George's whole body. A pint-sized Asian doctor walked over and pulled me aside.

"Are you Mrs. Johnson?" I barely whispered yes as I kept attempting to look at George but the doctor kept trying to block my view by turning me away.

"I'm Doctor Luke."

Then he hesitated, which really unnerved me.

He took my hand in his and said, "I'm sorry to say that your husband didn't make it. We did everything that we could think of but his heart gave out."

I felt faint, so the doctor directed me over to the nearest chair. I couldn't think straight. The room was spinning around me. The others started walking out of the room, and as they did one of the interns mumbled something about a corpse. How insensitive. Tears started trickling down my cheeks.

Doctor Luke yelled, "Get him out of here! And John, we will talk about this later."

That intern is going to become some kind of doctor. I felt sorry for his patients already. Oh my God, how could I tell my son about his dad? How are we going to survive?

"What happened?"

"From what I understand, he was hit by a taxi cab when he ran across the street to catch a bus. It was a hit and run that happened so fast that no one was able to get the tag number. The ambulance got there as fast as it could. I am so sorry for your loss."

"I want to see my George."

"Are you sure?"

"I, I think so." I stammered.

Doctor Luke walked me over to the bed, and turned the sheet back. George, who used to be a tall dark muscular man, looked like a shriveled man. I felt one of his cheeks. It was cold and rough. My voice was shaky as I started talking to him.

"George, oh my sweet baby George, I am so sorry. How could this happen to us? What am I going to do without you? What am I going to do with two kids?"

Earlier that day I had received my test results from the doctor's office and was waiting with excitement to tell George about this pregnancy. I was going to tell him after he got home from work. Sadly, he never had a chance to come home. The more I talked to him the more emotional I became. It was so sad to think that he would never know about this baby.

I laid my head down on his chest to check for a heartbeat, just in case the doctor was mistaken. Doctors aren't perfect you know. They make mistakes just like everybody else. But in this case, the doctor was right. There was no heartbeat, no pulse, no nothing.

"Don't leave me George! I don't know if I can make it alone in this crazy world! I love you! We need you!"

I was sobbing frantically as I tried to shake George. Doctor Luke walked up to me and pulled me off George. While he was pulling me away, I continued reaching out for George. My body was shaking violently as I yelled and screamed for George.

"Nurse, nurse, come here I need a sedative for Mrs. Johnson."

"No, I can't take a sedative, doctor. I'm pregnant and I don't want to hurt my baby," I said as I clenched my stomach.

A tall, lanky nurse came into the room and tried to talk me into calming down. She had a soothing tone, which helped a lot unlike nurse Wright's harsh tone.

"Mrs. Johnson, you have to calm down. You have a baby to think about. You don't want to put this baby in any jeopardy, do you?"

"No I don't, I'll try."

This whole thing happened out of the blue. I was completely caught off guard. Here one minute, gone the next. Nothing can ever be taken for granted. Nothing and no one, ever!

I hate this thing called death. It robs you by taking away the ones you love. My heart hurt immensely.

I didn't know what to do or where to go from there. I felt such a void buried in my heart and in my soul. A deep, deep hole that could never be filled. I was all alone. All alone without the only true love of my life, my wonderful, loveable George…

The Arrival

B rian had been devastated by his father's death. He withdrew from his friends and tried to withdraw from me but I didn't allow that to happen. I comforted him by expressing my feelings so that he would feel comfortable verbalizing his feelings. That way we could deal with our pain together.

I struggled to pay my bills by working as a payroll clerk at the Chase Brooklyn Bank on 5th Avenue. Even though I had only worked for them about six months before George passed away, the employees at this company were good to me. My colleagues collected hundreds of dollars to help me pay some bills, and sent cards and flowers. My manager even gave me a couple of days off with pay to try to get myself together. He wanted me to be as stress free as possible to avoid any complications with my unborn baby. And when it was time to return to work he wanted me to be able to focus on my job.

Several months later it was time for Bae George to make her appearance. I got up one weekend on a Saturday feeling the need to rearrange my apartment. I peeked in on Brian who was still soundly asleep. I had a piece of toast, some orange juice then started rearranging the little bit of furniture that we had in the living room. After about fifteen minutes, I started cramping. I started timing what felt like contractions then called the doctor and left a message with his answering service. He called me back and told me to go to the hospital he'd meet me there. I called Deja so she could keep an eye on Brian. As soon as I got off the phone, she was right there pounding on my door. I don't know why up to that point she didn't have a key.

"Bay! Oh my God! It's time for our little person to come into this world!" she said all alarmed. She looked so cute with her scarf wrapped around her braids. She had on a silk gold nightgown that was covered by her medium gold bathrobe. And of course her feathered slippers matched everything.

"Yep I think so too."

"Where's your bag?"

"It's right there," I said as I pointed to the bag near the door.

"Did you call the taxi cab yet?"

"No I was going to but stopped to let you in."

"Don't worry," she said as she walked over to the phone and started dialing.

"Oh!" I said holding my stomach.

"Bay, hold on, the taxi cab is on the way. Come on, I'll help you downstairs. Just lock the door, give me the keys and I'll come back up and wake Brian up to fill him in. Miles already rearranged his room for Brian's stay, so don't worry about him, he's in good hands."

"You know that I have no doubt about that at all. Hey Deja, you know you shouldn't go downstairs dressed like that."

"Girl, these people know that I don't care what they think about my attire," Deja said.

"I know, but it's not lady like to go outside in your nightgown."

"Bay, you are wasting your breath because you know that I am going to do what I want."

"You're right, miss hardhead," I said with a little smile on my face.

I locked the door, and gave her my keys. She took my bag from me when we got into the elevator.

"Oh God, I don't know why we got into this elevator, the way it gets stuck sometimes."

"Deja! Don't jinx me, crazy girl!"

"Sorry Bay, I wasn't thinking. See, we're on the first floor now. Phew."

Deja walked me out to the street where amazingly the taxi was waiting for us. This was not the norm because we normally had to wait a while for a taxi in this neighborhood. She gave the bag to the taxi cab driver and also stuffed some money into my hand.

"Deja."

"Bay, I told you I wanted to help out. These taxis can be expensive sometimes, that's why we always take the subway," she whispered.

Deja kissed my cheek and said, "I love you sis. Take care and have a safe delivery. I can't wait to see my new little niece. You know that I want a niece but I'll be cliché and say that I just want a healthy baby. Call me."

"I will. Love you too."

Everything went well with my natural delivery and Bae George was a healthy seven pound six ounce baby. I was only in labor about four hours thank goodness. She was so tiny and so beautiful. I expected a dark baby, but she was almost white with a carpet of dark hair that covered her head. She had fat cheeks and pouty lips.

After we got settled into our private room, I called Deja. She was so excited that she wanted to talk to Bae George over the phone. Then Brian and Miles jumped on the phone and expressed their excitement. After I hung up the phone, I could only stare at Bae George and pray to God.

"Thank you God for this beautiful healthy baby. I am so sorry that she will never know her father. George would have just eaten her up. He would have been beside himself. He would have had both the son and the daughter he always wanted. Now he will never know about her. Please help me to be strong enough to raise both of them alone. You know it's not easy being a single parent. But I know that as long as I have you and Deja in my corner, I will be all right. And God, I love you."

A few moments later the door opened and a nurse walked in.

"Hello. How are you feeling? Is there anything that you need?"

"I am feeling just a little sore and a little tired but other than that I can't complain."

"That's good. I came to get your baby and take her to the nursery. Bae George, that's a name that I've never heard before. It's kinda cute."

"Thanks. Her name is a combination of my first name and her dad George's first name. I don't want to let her go, can she stay a little while longer?"

"I'm sorry but it's time for us to put all of the babies back in the nursery. We'll take good care of her. You'll get to see her first thing in the morning. If you need anything just buzz for a nurse."

As she reached out her arms for Bae George, I kissed my baby gently on her cheeks and on her eyes.

"Bae George, you taste good. Your cheeks are so soft. Mommy loves you."

After the nurse left with my baby, I fell asleep.

Bae George's birth helped Brian bounce back to being a normal kid again. He was enamored with her. He had to feed her, change her diaper, brush her hair, and change her clothes. Whatever had to be done, he felt he was the one who had to do it. That didn't leave much for me to do, so I had a chance to get a lot of rest. Besides, what he didn't do, Miles and Deja took care of. I just love my family. Sometimes life shuffles your cards in different directions, but I believe that God makes sure that they get shuffled back into the right order.

Several weeks later I went back to work. Brian did exceptionally well in school that year despite having to adjust to a more stringent daily routine.

Every morning on our way out, we took Bae George to the babysitter's. Mrs. Collins was an amicable older lady in her late fifties who lived a few blocks from our apartment. She was a short, stout black woman who always had a smile on her face. She had already raised her children and some grandchildren and loved kids so much that she didn't mind keeping other people's kids to help them out.

On any given day she could be seen outside playing with the kids or walking them home from school. She walked some kids to their apartment. Others like Brian and Miles, she kept until the parents got home from work. What a blessing. She didn't even charge me the asking price for babysitting. Thank God because I don't know what I would have done. Here she was with all of these kids and she still managed to spend quality time with each and every one of them. She even kept my kids late sometimes without charging me extra. At times I would arrive late because those trains never seem to be on time. And rush hour, forget it! Other times I was late because I had to make a stop at the A&P to pick up a few items.

After dropping off Bae George, I would walk Brian and Miles down the block close to the school where I could see the other school kids walking. There were also school crossing guards down that block since there was another school across the street from theirs.

I always stood there and watched them walk down a couple of blocks, then I was off to the train station on Smith and 9th Street to catch the A train to my job.

Each day after work I picked up the children from the babysitter's. Brian and Miles disliked going because they thought that they were grown enough to stay home alone for a couple of hours after school. But what they didn't realize was that I was a protective, nervous mother who didn't really trust anyone. Miles was like a son to me and I treated him like one. I was afraid something could happen, and that they would have to deal with the situation by themselves.

After picking up the children, we would see Miles to his apartment. Deja worked weird hours so there were days when Miles stayed at our place for a while. I always looked over their homework to see if they finished it. I knew that there were times when Brian and Miles got sidetracked and I would be up all night helping with homework. Afterwards the kids would eat, and then take a bath. Depending on the time, the kids would have a chance to watch some television shows. When they were watching television, Bae George was always right beside them in her playpen. Of course she didn't know what she was watching. She was oblivious to everything. Brian didn't care, he loved having her in the same room near him at all times.

The kids' bedtime was always around 8:00 p.m. Brian and I always knelt by his bed, while I held Bae George, and said a prayer. If Miles were still there at that time, he would join us in prayer too. By the time the kids finally fell asleep, it was late and pretty much time for me to go to bed too. But despite this I tried to make sure I at least had some time to myself to collect my thoughts for the day...

The Departure

Something tragic happened in April of the following year that shook up the entire neighborhood. Things like that just didn't happen in our neighborhood. Everything started off normal that somber morning. Then I received a call from Deja.

"Girl, quick, turn to channel 5!"

I walked over to the television with the phone in my hand and turned to channel 5. The broadcast was already in progress.

"We are strongly urging the residents of the 747-749 Henry Street block of the Red Hook projects to be on high alert this morning. Around 3 a.m. this morning, the household of the Reese family, of 747 Henry Street, was tragically shaken up. The husband and father, Jack Reese, apparently awoke to the sound of someone opening one of his dresser drawers."

"He tried to pull the element of surprise on the two masked men who appeared to be pilfering through his belongings and jumped out of the bed. His wife Solange saw him scuffle with the intruders so she picked up a lamp and tried to hit one of them. Then according to Mrs. Solange Reese, the unthinkable happened. During the scuffle a loud shot rang out and Mrs. Reese saw her tall husband's body go limp."

"After they shot him, the intruders ran out of the apartment. Mrs. Reese followed and locked the door. She then ran over to tend to her husband. He was alive but was barely breathing. She made sure that their daughter was okay then called the police."

"But by the time the police and ambulance arrived, Jack Reese had already expired. His wife, Solange Reese, and his five-year-old daughter, Reena Reese, survive him. At this moment, the police do not have any suspects. These two seemed to have completely vanished into thin air, which leads police to believe that they live very close by."

"We are advising residents to make sure that all of the doors are locked. Those of you who live on the first floor need to also make sure that the windows are locked. And keep an eye open for any strangers in your neighborhood or anyone who looks out of place. Mrs. Reese was not able to give the police an accurate description of the intruders because it was too dark in the apartment. This is Jeanne Cartel, Channel 5, Eyewitness News."

After the broadcast, I turned the television off. I knew that because of this brief pause, we would be running a little late.

"Oh Deja! I'm scared," I said into the phone, "there were two adults living there, and it's just me and you here!"

"Girl, try not to worry too much about it. This was probably an isolated incident. Those Reeses were quiet people who kept to themselves. Those guys probably knew the victim and figured he had something they wanted."

"I don't know Deja."

"Bay! Come on! Keep it together, you'll be all right! Stop worrying! You worry too much! I just wanted you to know what was going on before you left for work this morning. That's all, ok?"

I tried to remain calm as I said, "Ok, thanks Deja. I'll be careful, and I'll speak with you when I get home this evening."

"Ok, bye Bay."

That Deja is something else. She seemed to know everything that was going on, and made sure that I knew about it too. Sometimes I think she's sort of like my guardian. What a friend… What a true friend.

The rest of that day I couldn't help thinking about that poor Reese family. The way that I had lost George was hard enough, but I couldn't even begin to imagine losing him due to murder! How devastating! This family had always kept to themselves, which made me wonder if they had friends or family who would be there for them.

Several weeks after the murder, Deja dropped a bombshell on me. I had just arrived home from work and was still trying to rebound from the murder of the Reese man, the weather was drizzly and dreary, and her news just did not help. It was bad timing.

There was a soft knock on the door.

"Just a minute," I said as I looked through the peephole and pulled open the door.

"Hi Bay," Deja said as she kissed me on the cheek and walked passed me.

"Hi Deja."

She sat down on my couch and nervously shook one of her long, golden-brown crossed legs. She was holding a glass of wine that she seemed to have downed all in one gulp. The boys were in Brian's room doing their homework, well, at least that's what they told me. They seemed to be talking and giggling a little too much to be doing homework. Bae George was on the living room floor, playing with her toys.

"Deja, what's going on? In all of the years that I've known you, I don't think that I've ever seen you look this disheartened."

"Bay, you need to sit down."

I didn't like the sound of that, but I had no choice if I wanted to know what was going on.

"Bay, there's no easy way to say this, so I'll just come out with it. Miles and I are gonna be moving soon."

My heart started pounding so hard that I thought it would come right through my skin. My mouth dropped and my lips started to tremble as I replied, "Moving? Where, why?"

"We'll be moving down to Jacksonville, Florida this summer. Right after school lets out."

"Jacksonville? Why would you leave your beloved New York to move to Florida?"

"Because that's where Miles' father lives and he wants us to be with him. Since Miles will be a teenager soon he wants to play a bigger role in his life. I guess it's not too late for him to teach Miles how to be a man. I think better late than never. It also looks like there might be a chance for us to get back together. Bay, he finally divorced Kim."

I stood up and said, "Get back together after all of these years? What kind of sense does that make? I don't want you to move down there based solely on promises that could turn out to be empty promises again. I love you too much. You're my best friend, my sister. I don't want him to have a chance to hurt you again. Are you sure that he is divorced?"

Deja stood up and paced back and forth.

"Bay, I have to look at this as positively as I can and take a chance for Miles' sake. I'm sure that if Big Miles said that he divorced Kim then he must have done so. Why would he want to lie to me?"

"I hope he is on the up and up this time, but Deja, you'll be so far away. I lost my George and now I am losing you. I don't know if I can handle this."

Tears started streaming down my cheeks.

"How long have you been thinking about this?"

"We had been talking about it for a couple of weeks. But the decision was made today. Especially with the murder that happened in this neighborhood. It did not unnerve me because you know that I'm not afraid of anything, but it unnerved Miles' father."

Deja also was crying as she walked over and wiped my tears. She hugged me and we sat back down on the couch.

"Deja, what am I gonna do without you?"

"Bay, why don't you come with us?"

"You know I can't do that."

"Why not? You can stay with me and Miles until you get a job and get situated."

Deja raised her long black eyelashes in hopes that I would acquiesce. She didn't want to leave me either, that's why her decision was so difficult.

"Thanks Deja, but you know I don't like to be a burden on anyone. Besides at this point in my life, I'm not in any position to leave New York."

"Oh shucks, ok, but I want you to know that I will keep in touch. And if you change your mind, the offer is always open. You hear me girl?" She said as she held my face up to hers. She wanted to make sure that I knew she meant every single word of what she said.

"Yep, I'll keep that in mind."

We hugged again.

"I love you, little sis."

"I love you too, big sis."

This always tickled me because we were only about a year apart but Deja always acted as if she was my big sister instead of the reverse.

Months later, when it came time for Deja and Miles to move, I had a sharp twinge of pain deep down in the pit of my stomach. I hate good-byes. They are so painful and sometimes seem so final. Just like how death feels final.

It was a bright sunny morning in mid June when it came time to say good-bye. I'd hoped the fact that the sun was shining on such a gloomy day symbolized something positive for all of us in our uncertain future. The days leading up to this moment were almost unbearable.

I had to stay away from Deja's apartment because watching her pack up her things was so depressing. But I guess it must have been hard for her too. She was more of a sister to me than any real biological sister could have ever been!

For the third time in my life, it felt like someone was ripping and tearing a piece of my heart right out from my body. First my mom then my beloved husband, George, and now my one and only best friend in the whole wide world was leaving me but in a different capacity.

After the movers went downstairs to load the last box onto the moving van, Deja came over to my place. We exchanged our good-byes while we stood in my doorway. We both knew that if she came in it would be that much more difficult to let go. Deja was dressed in a white shorts set that had big black polka dots all over it, and she was hooked up with a matching purse and black leather sandals. Her eyebrows were neatly arched and she was wearing her favorite purple passion lipstick. One might think overkill, but to Deja this was just her style.

We stood there in silence while we looked at each other for I don't know how long. I could feel the tears starting to form in my eyes, and I noticed that Deja's tears were already sliding down her beautiful face.

"Well," Deja said, "I guess this is it."

She stood back a little as if she was afraid to hug me good-bye.

"Yep, I guess this is it."

"You have all of my information so don't lose it! Remember if you don't want to move to Florida you and the kids can always come down for vacation, ok?"

I could barely speak, so in response I just shook my head yes. I reached out and pulled Deja towards me and hugged her tight because

I didn't ever want to forget her touch. We embraced for a minute then kissed each other on the cheek.

Deja broke the silence when she said, "You take good care of yourself Bay. I'm gonna miss all of you. Please promise me that you will keep in touch."

"I promise. Love you Deja. I hope that everything works out for you. I really mean it. I pray that you get what you are looking for."

I stood there in a daze just looking at her. The water in my eyes was stinging so badly that I could barely see her. Deja put her right hand up and waved good-bye. I did the same as she turned around and walked away. She didn't look back. I softly closed the door and stood with my back against it for a few minutes while I continued sobbing uncontrollably.

Dennis

The years flew by and I managed to keep our lives in some kind of order. Or at least I tried to anyway. Bae George was in pre-kindergarten, and Brian was now quite a nice-looking young man. He had just turned seventeen during the summer of 1984 and was ready to run the streets. We had also heard from Deja on and off, which was always a pleasure.

Ever since Miles left years earlier, Brian had some difficulty reaching out to make new friends. He knew that I liked most of his friends, but there was this one friend, Dennis, who I didn't really care for. He came from a generational welfare family of about twelve kids and counting, and his mother never seemed to keep an eye on him, or on any of her other kids for that matter. And the father or I should say fathers were never around.

Since Dennis was one of the middle children, he preferred to hang out with his older brothers instead of hanging out with the younger ones. This Mendez family always seemed to disrupt things and wreak havoc. The girls were ruthless and cutthroat just like the boys. If you looked at them the wrong way, that was grounds for a fight. They were a gang of bullies who hung out together and fought dirty. These kids spent a lot of time in and out of juvenile hall. At such a young age they were obviously headed down the wrong path.

The times when Dennis was in my presence, he had always been disrespectful. His language was so filthy and he didn't care who heard it. I had long ago put a stop to his coming by our apartment, but I suspected that Brian might have hung out with him on the sly from time to time anyway. Even though Dennis was a little younger than

Brian, he thought he was grown. I guess he felt he had something to prove since he always hung out all hours of the night with his thuggish big brothers.

One evening while Brian and I were playing the game Kerplunk the subject of Dennis came up. Even though this was kind of a kid's game, it was my favorite game and Brian never turned me down when I wanted to revisit a childhood game. I was convinced that I had to keep warning him about his association with Dennis. He gave me the same response that he always gave.

"Ah mom, come on lighten up. Dennis is cool. He just tries to act tough to keep up with his brothers. He's really an okay guy deep down inside. I just know it."

I paused, looked Brian directly in his eyes and said, "Brian, that boy is bad news. As a matter of fact that whole family is bad news. I told you to stay away from them."

He attempted to interject but I put my hand up and said, "Don't interrupt me. Be quiet and let me finish."

I felt the need to be stern so that he could see the seriousness of what I had to say.

"Mothers, or should I say good mothers, can sense things that their children don't have the wisdom and foresight to sense. Trust me, I have been out there. And I have learned and experienced a lot. Give me credit for what I know. You have a lot to learn, and as a parent it's my job to teach you, but you gotta listen. You don't know everything. Goodness gracious!"

I tried to drive home the point because I had just started working a second job a couple of nights a week, and I needed to feel assured that Brian had a clear head on his shoulders. He not only had himself to look after, but Bae George as well.

I felt exasperated because it was becoming obvious to me that Brian was just not hearing me. Even though he was now a young man of seventeen, he still had a certain innocence about himself, and I wanted to always be there to protect him. He was at that sassy teenage stage where he thought that he knew more than I did. Despite that he basically was a good kid who had a stubborn streak in him. He was truly a chip off of the old block. Not my block of course but his dad's.

"Ok, ok mom. You worry too much."

Then Brian turned his attention back to the game. But I didn't want to play anymore because I started having bad vibes and I had no idea why. I tried to shake them off by playing with Bae George. She is truly a gift and a constant reminder of her father. She had his pretty hazel eyes, long eyelashes and his beautiful smile. I'll never forget his smile. Never… Her skin has a creamy glow to it and she has short, shiny brown hair, which I kept styled in candy curls. She also has a birthmark on the left side of her neck that looked like a little cherry.

Although my skin's lighter and my brown eyes are darker, Brian, on the other hand, looks more like me. Only he's brown skinned and has light brown eyes. He also has his own one-of-a-kind smile. The kind of smile that exposed all his sparkling white teeth. He is gregarious and sometimes *overtly* friendly, which caused all kinds of people to flock to him. All of the young people in the neighborhood wanted to be in his presence. Bae George is the complete opposite. She is more of an introvert. She's shy and chooses to stay close by my side…

I struggled so much throughout the years that I usually only managed to buy a chicken for the holidays. I actually started slacking up on the holidays because I started losing interest. I decided that this would be our last Thanksgiving holiday because I felt thankful everyday and didn't see the reason behind waiting one day in the year to celebrate being thankful. When I talked to Brian about it, he agreed and said that he understood my reason.

This year I was able to save up enough money to buy a small turkey, dressing and other fixings. I cooked the turkey the best way that I knew how. And with a little help from Betty Crocker I also managed to bake a cherry pie from scratch. The turkey was a little dry, but the kids were content and they enjoyed Thanksgiving dinner, which really pleased me.

Afterwards we were sitting on the floor watching football when the phone rang.

"Hello?" I inquired.

"Hey girl!"

"Deja!"

"How have you been Bay?" Deja asked.

"Fine! Oh Deja I miss you. How are things going with you all?"

"Oh Bay, it's so nice down here. You would love the weather. When are you coming down?"

"Soon Deja, soon."

"Bay, you've been telling me that for several years now."

"I know but I have been so busy working two jobs."

"Come on Bay, you need to take a breather because before you know it, one day you'll look up and more years will have gone by. I guess I'm gonna have to come up there to see you all."

"No you won't. I promise I'll come visit you soon, ok?"

"You sure you promise?"

"Yes Deja, I'm sure. I'll see what I can do in the next few months."

"Now you know I'll send you the money, if that is what's holding you back."

"I know and I appreciate it. But I don't want to put you out like that so I'll save up the money. So tell me what's up down there in sunny Florida?"

"Things are going well. Miles has adjusted to the South and is doing well in school. His dad and I are getting along great. We're now living in a three-bedroom apartment in a new high-rise building in downtown Jacksonville. It's close to everything! The river walk, the malls, the airport, movies, clubs, you name it. That third bedroom is for you and Bae George, you know. And Brian can stay with Miles. Remember what I told you?"

"Yes Deja, I remember. What about work? How is the job market?"

"The jobs are plentiful here. I didn't have a problem getting one and you won't either."

We talked and gossiped for a while. I gave her the scoop on what was going on in the neighborhood since the last time we'd spoken. Miles and Brian also had a chance to talk and then it was time to get off of the phone. I didn't want to run up her long distance bill.

"Deja, I promise to call you next month. Ok?"

"All right, I guess that's a good idea. We need to talk more often. And Bay…take care of yourself and the kids."

"I promise I will."

"I love you, Bay."

"I love you too sis."

After Thanksgiving, the days and nights flew by quickly. It was December now and time for me to go Christmas shopping. This too was going to be the last Christmas celebration because I had many questions about this holiday and about the Bible that my priest couldn't answer. As a matter of fact, he seemed to be altogether avoiding me. So I guess I'll have to go somewhere else to get my answers.

I'd put the shopping off for as long as I could. I made a budget for each child, and I promised myself that I would stick to it. With Brian having become a young man, it was now more difficult to find something to buy for him. His preferences had changed and were now more mature, so he no longer desired little, inexpensive things. This year he wanted a car. Even though it would be a used car, it was still an expense out of my immediate budget. I was saving the money from my second job for this holiday's gifts.

I wanted to send Deja something too, but decided that she would be just as happy with a card and a picture of us. She knew that I really couldn't afford a gift, and besides it was the thought that counted anyway.

The only thing that Bae George wanted was a Barbie camper. She said that way Barbie and Skipper would be able to go on trips. Ok whatever…

Brian's Misplaced Trust

It was Saturday evening, December 8th when I packed my two tote bags to get ready to go to work. Brian and Bae George were in the living room eating potato chips and watching television when I walked in.

"Brian, I'm getting ready to leave for work."

Bae George ran over to me, hugged my legs and said, "I don't want you to go mommy."

I bent down and said, "I know baby, but I have to. Besides you get to stay up late with your big brother. Isn't that cool?"

She changed her tune, started hopping up and down and said, "That's right. I get to stay up with Bri Bri! See you later mommy."

I bent down to kiss her and then she sat back down on the floor. She was so cute in her wonder woman nightgown.

Brian walked over to me, kissed my cheek and said, "Mom, I see the worry in your face. Go on to work and stop worrying. When have I ever let you down? You know I love Bae to death and would never let anything happen to her."

"I know. Ok, gotta go. Call you when I get there. And don't forget to put Bae George in bed after she falls asleep."

"I got it," Brian said as he guided me to the door.

"I love you two."

"Love you!" Bae George yelled all the while keeping her eyes glued to the television set.

"Love you too mom," Brian said as he closed the door behind me and locked it.

I arrived at work around 9 p.m. that evening and called home to check on the kids. "Mom, everything is ok. Bae George is asleep in her bed, and I am sitting here on the couch watching *The Jeffersons*."

"Good, if I get a chance I'll call you on my break."

So I went on with my work of processing medical claims at the twenty-four-hour Manhattan City Medical Center.

Meanwhile minutes later, back at home the phone rang.

"Hello?" Brian inquired.

"Hey Brian, what ya doing tonight?"

"Dennis?"

"Yep."

"I have to watch my sister while mom's at work. Why?"

"Because the guys and I are gonna play basketball."

"This time of the night?"

"Yep. Come on, don't be a sissy. The lights are on in the park and I'm sure someone already shoveled the snow off of the court. And we bring sand for traction so that we don't slide too much."

"I know. Come on Dennis you don't understand, I can't tonight."

"My sister Maria will come over and keep an eye on your sister. We won't be out long. Come on Brian."

"Dennis, I don't know. I'm not even supposed to really be hanging out with you. Besides I don't want to disappoint my mom. She expects me to be here taking care of Bae George."

"Brian, I promise, we won't be gone long. Come on. Take a chance in life for once, would ya? We'll be out and back probably before your mom even calls again to check up on you two. Besides Maria won't mind. We'll be right over."

"But–"

Approximately six minutes later Dennis, who is a tall curly headed brown skinned Puerto Rican and his look-alike sister Maria arrived at the apartment. Brian was reluctant to go but felt pressured because he didn't want to be known as a sissy. This caused him to lose all of the good reasoning that was instilled in him from his mother.

"Maria, take good care of my sister. I will be back in a few," Brian said.

Brian and Dennis left the building, basketball in hand, on their way to the park. Or so that is what Brian thought. They met up with the others on their way.

"Brian, the plans have changed for a minute. We have to make a quick stop at James' place first. Come on," Dennis said.

Brian was not at all enthused about this but went along anyway. The other guys were older and lived in the same neighborhood. One was as old as twenty. Brian felt uneasy hanging with them but liked the adventure of playing basketball that late knowing that he'd be home way before his mother's next call.

"Hey Dennis, this isn't James' place. What's going on?"

"Shush Brian," Dennis said as he and the two other guys tried prying open the door to someone's apartment.

"Uh Dennis I'm going back home. This doesn't feel right to me. I don't think we should be here."

"Too late Brian, you're not going anywhere," Joe said.

He was the oldest and the biggest one hanging out with them. As Brian attempted to leave, Joe grabbed and jerked him into the apartment after the others jimmied the door open with a crowbar and walked in. Joe continued pulling Brian with him while the others tiptoed around the apartment with a flashlight. Brian resisted but to no avail. Joe was a lot bigger and stronger. Brian was afraid of the whole situation and just wanted to go home.

He now understood why his mom had found reason to continually warn him about associating with Dennis. He indeed was bad news. Brian started thinking about the murder that had happened years ago to the Reese family. He now figured that Dennis' family probably had something to do with it. The sound of gunfire brought Brian out of his thoughts and he looked around and saw everyone running in various directions.

"Pow, pow! You better get outta here!" Bellowed the resident and his gun.

This time the boys had met their match. This man was determined that nothing would ever happen to his family. He was sick and tired of hearing about the recent burglaries in the projects. As far as he was concerned he worked too hard to achieve his goals and possessions and wasn't going to let some punks screw up his life. The whole neighborhood knew he was a hard-working man, and to some this equated to money, money and more money. His wife and kids always dressed decently and never wore drabby or dingy clothes. A lot of the teenagers in their neighborhood were jealous of them.

This resident, Marcus, sensed this and made sure that in order to take care of his family in that fashion, he had to get a gun for their protection. Well that night it served its purpose. He managed to drive the thugs away but believed that he might have shot one of them. He didn't want to kill anybody. He just wanted to scare them away. Although it was dark at the time of the shooting, he believed he saw that Dennis Mendez boy and thought that the other boy looked like Brian Johnson. But later he dismissed that thought because the whole neighborhood knew Brian was a good kid. There was never any dirt circulating about him. He came from a good family.

"Run man run!" Dennis shouted. The snow on the ground made it difficult for them to run, they kept slipping and sliding.

"Hey Dennis, I've been shot!" Joe yelled.

He clutched his stomach and fell backwards in the snow.

Dennis was still running and yelled, "Come on Joe stop playing around!"

When Dennis didn't receive an answer he turned around and saw that Joe was down in the snow. Mike was standing over him trying to help him.

Brian still heard the others yelling but he continued running home. He was scared out of his wits.

"He's dead. Come on Mike, we gotta get outta here! Hey where's Brian?" Dennis asked.

They looked and saw a shadow up ahead running towards their part of the neighborhood.

"Come on Mike, we gotta shut him up before he rats on us," Dennis said.

Brian was about two-thirds of the way home when the guys caught up to him. They ganged up on him and beat him senseless. There was blood everywhere.

Brian was down in the snow on his back as he pleaded, "Please stop Dennis. I…I promise I won't say anything."

These were his last words as Dennis swung the crowbar like a baseball bat and bashed Brian on the front left side of his head. The blow was fatal. Blood gushed out from this side of Brian's brain and he immediately died.

Mike couldn't believe his eyes as he knelt down and checked for a pulse. When he didn't feel one he said, "Dennis you killed him man. You killed him!"

"So what. At least he can't rat on us now," Dennis said coldly.

"How can you be so heartless? Who said he was gonna to rat on us?"

"Mike you better shut up. You helped me beat him up so you are just as guilty. You are an accessory to murder! I trust that you will keep this to yourself, right?"

Dennis smirked as he playfully elbowed Mike in the stomach. Mike tried to smile but was feeling nervous about the whole situation. This was the first time that one of their burglaries had resulted in deaths.

During Dennis' brothers' burglaries, they didn't have a problem killing if the situation got out of control. Mike started to fear for his life. The burglaries used to be fun and exciting, but not anymore. In all of the years that he had known Dennis, he had never seen him this way. Dennis had totally lost it.

"Right, I…I'm your bud. I won't say anything." Mike stammered.

"That's right. I know you'll keep your trap shut!"

"Uh-huh." Mike conceded.

"Quick now help me get his jacket and his sneakers off. We'll make it look like he was robbed."

They took off Brian's sneakers and jacket and tossed them in a nearby dumpster, then ran home…

Bad Influences

My darkness began in the wee hours of a dismal, snowy morning on December 9th, 1984 while I was on my way home from my second job. I needed the job desperately because of my outrageous bills. And I needed extra money because Christmas was coming up. I didn't want to disappoint Brian again. I had promised that I would try to buy him an old '66 black Mustang he'd been eyeing.

I desperately wanted my own transportation, because the walk from the Smith & 9th train station was on the other side of the tracks, and quite a distance from the projects. After exiting the train station, I walked across Court Street and Clinton Street then under the expressway. In the slushy, dirty snow I crossed Columbia Street over to Dwight Street. I walked passed the library, passed Scotty's barbershop and further down passed the A&P. My mom used to collect S&H green stamps at that A&P so that she could get free merchandise.

Up ahead I saw the headlights of a car that turned off one of the side streets. Other than that, there wasn't any activity going on at this time of the morning. I guess it was too cold and too early for any activity.

As I walked right into the entrance of the projects, I had a hard time holding onto the two tote bags that I normally take to work with me. They kept slipping out of my hands and falling. They were so heavy because of all of the magazines and bills I always carried with me. I preferred reading my magazines instead of staring at people on the train.

As I was bending down to pick them up again, I looked up and noticed something up ahead. I started to walk towards it passed several buildings on my left and the park on my right. When I put my bags down to take a closer look, I discovered that it was a young black man laying still and he had been stripped of his coat and shoes.

My heart started beating wildly when I knelt down and turned him over. There was blood everywhere!

"Oh my God! It's it's–!"

I started shaking him in hopes of waking him. I checked for a pulse but was quivering so badly that I didn't know whether or not I felt one.

"Help! Help! Somebody help me!" I screamed.

I screamed and screamed, but there wasn't anyone around to hear me. I stood up in hopes of running into one of the buildings to yell for help, but as I proceeded to turn I slipped on the blood in the mushy snow, fell back, and smashed the back of my head against the slippery snowy pavement…

My Darkness

I opened my eyes, looked around and saw nothing but white walls. Oh my goodness, where am I? My head was pounding and it hurt so immensely. I was feeling groggy as I yelled for someone to help me.

To my dismay in walked nurse Wright. She stood on the right side of the hospital bed and said, "What's all the yelling about? What do you want?"

I stammered, "Wh… what am I doing here?"

I could sense from the jump that she seemed to have the same attitude she had years ago which befuddled me.

"Don't you remember?"

I shook my head no as I looked around and saw that I was hooked up to an IV. It had clear liquid dripping down into a vein in my left arm.

"Where's my son?"

I vaguely remembered seeing him earlier but couldn't remember where.

"Your son, Brian's the name right?"

"Yes, please tell me where he is," I said weakly.

"Well I hate to be the bearer of bad news but your son died hours ago," Nurse Wright said nonchalantly as she grabbed my arm and started checking my blood pressure.

"What…what are you saying? Not my Brian."

"Yes you heard me right the first time. He's dead. He's gone!"

She made a motion with her fingers to signify poof as in disappeared, no longer here. How could she be so heartless, so cruel?

"No, no!"

I wanted to choke her.

I started screaming and squirming which only made things worse. At that moment a doctor walked in and restrained me.

"Doctor this patient has flipped! I suggest we put her in restraints."

"Nurse Wright, that sounds like a quick fix. Come over here and help me take care of that."

She held me down while the doctor went out to get a sedative. Then nurse Wright put her ugly mug right in my face. I don't think that I'd ever felt this helpless and this vulnerable in all of my life.

She said snidely, "I suggest you calm down and you betta not say a word to anybody about how our little conversation went."

I was stunned.

"Why are you acting like this? I've never done anything to you, I don't even personally know you."

"Project people like you make me sick," she retorted. "You give our race a bad name. Just because you're light-skinned with long hair don't mean that you ain't black. You ain't betta than anybody else living in those projects."

I wonder what her problem is. She sounds a little unstable to me.

"I work so hard to have the best things that life has to offer. This includes insurance. I'm a nurse and you have betta insurance coverage than I have! How do you rate?"

I mustered up enough strength to reply.

"I'll have you know that I work hard for the best things in life too, and just because I live in the projects doesn't mean that I am on any government assistance, and if this were the case, that would be my business not yours. Being on assistance doesn't make someone less than a human being. We all might need a little help from time to time."

"Humph, not me! I will never live in the projects with the rest of you people. Never."

"Well honey, you need a reality check because one day you just might have to eat those words."

This nonsense was not making me feel any better. Who does she think she is? So what she's a nurse and doesn't have to live in the projects! Big deal! That doesn't make her better than I am.

When the doctor returned, nurse Wright was standing by my bed with her arms crossed and had a smile on her face as if nothing ever happened. When the doctor saw that I had calmed down, he said he didn't want to take any chances and decided to give me a mild sedative anyway.

"I don't know what happened here but nurse Wright I have to give you credit for calming my patient down. Thanks, we need more good nurses like you. I'll be in again later to check her chart."

He patted her on the shoulder and walked out of the room. I could tell by their body language that this wasn't where he wanted to pat her. She smirked again at me on her way out of the room. She wanted to remind me of who had the upper hand and who had control over my destiny. How dare she? I softly cried until the sedative took effect...

Chief De Marco

uring my brief stay at the hospital, I was at my wits end trying to find out about Brian. And oh my goodness, if something happened to Brian then where's Bae George?

I didn't have to wait long because the next day the Chief of police, Chief De Marco from the Brooklyn 223rd precinct paid me a visit. He is a tall, stocky Italian man who has thick black eyebrows, dark brown eyes, and a burly mustache.

He sat down on the stiff yellow plastic chair that he dragged across the floor to the left side of my hospital bed. Then extended his hand out to me as he said, "Mrs. Johnson, I am Chief De Marco from the 223rd precinct. I am sorry about your son, Brian."

"So…so it's really true? M…my son is dead. This isn't all a dream?" I stammered.

He shook his head and said, "I'm afraid not."

He told me what the police investigation had determined. I was so upset, because Brian knew not to go out of the apartment that time of night. I just couldn't understand the whole thing because he would have never willingly left his sister at home alone. Everything was so surreal.

"Where's my daughter, Bae George?"

"She is at your neighbor Janice's apartment. Your son had identification on him, that's how we located your apartment. When we arrived there the door was ajar, so we walked in and found your daughter sleeping soundly in her bed. It didn't look like anything had been disturbed. So we went out into the hallway and knocked on a couple of doors until someone opened their door. It was your neighbor Janice."

"She had no idea about what was going on, and stated that she didn't see nor hear anything. As far as she knew the kids remained home after you left for work. She didn't hear any voices in the hallway or any doors closing. But she also stated that she was in her back room, and it is hard to hear things going on in the hallway from back there. She was concerned about Brian, you, and your daughter. She offered to watch your daughter until you came home. I was apprehensive at first, but when I saw the way that your daughter responded to her, I knew that she must be a regular visitor, a friend or both."

"Thank you Chief De Marco. You are very perceptive. Janice is a good choice."

I couldn't help thinking that if Deja were here, she would have, well she would have been the first choice, but …

Janice called me a couple of hours before my release that evening.

"Hi Bailey, it's Janice. You doing okay?"

"Yes thank you. I appreciate you looking after Bae George."

"She's no problem. I'll keep her a few more days until you feel good enough to get her."

"Thanks. I'll call you when I leave the hospital."

Upon my release from the hospital that evening, Chief De Marco arrived to take me to the morgue to get a positive identification on Brian. This was a very difficult thing for me to do.

When we arrived at the Rest Easy Memorial morgue on Prospect Avenue, I hesitated before going in.

"Are you sure that you are up to this Mrs. Johnson?" Chief De Marco asked as he tightly held my hand.

"I think so." It wasn't going to be real to me until I saw Brian for myself.

Once we walked inside, the verification process did not take long. After I positively identified Brian, I had this queasy feeling in the pit of my stomach. I turned and ran out of the morgue and regurgitated in the grass around the side of the building. Chief De Marco followed me, but not before he got a wet paper towel for me to use to wipe my mouth when I finished. That was kind of him.

"Mrs. Johnson, I am so sorry. People think that police officers aren't capable of having a heart, but I disagree. I've seen so much out there, and yes a lot of it can harden an officer's heart, but proper prospective keeps me grounded. Are you going to be okay?"

"Uh-huh."

He drove me home and made sure that I had everything that I needed for the night. This was truly unusual, not only because he was a stranger and a police officer, but also because he was a guy. I couldn't help but to think that his wife must be a very lucky woman.

"Mrs. Johnson…"

"Please call me Bailey," I said as I steadied myself against the refrigerator.

"Okay Bailey, I want you to have my card in case you have any questions, or in case you just need someone to talk to."

He must have sensed that I was all alone. I could see it in his eyes.

"I have daughters your age and I pride myself on being there for them. For some reason I am drawn to you. I guess it's because you kind of remind me of my beautiful daughter Rebecca."

He took my hand in his and said, "I promise you, Bailey, that I will get the people who are responsible for your son's murder. I promise."

"Chief De Marco, thank you very much for everything," I said to him before he walked out of my apartment.

After I closed the door behind him, I knew that I was in no position to see Bae George so I called Janice to check on her, replaced the phone on the hook, and cried…

The Funeral

Brian's funeral was held on a bitter cold morning that following weekend. I was still in shock, and not thinking clearly. I don't even know why I didn't contact Deja. She might have been able to help me get through this horrible period in my life.

So as not to attract any unwanted attention, the funeral took place at an undisclosed location. Only a few people were there, which is the way that I wanted it. Even in death I wanted Brian all to myself. I'm numb. First mom, then George, and now my baby Brian. Oh God please help me, I lost my baby. That is so unfair. He was so young. He had his whole life ahead of him.

I thought I was going to pass out at the burial site, but managed to compose myself for Bae George's sake. She was pretty in her black frilly dress as she stood by my side sobbing lightly.

After Brian was laid to rest, it was time for us to go. I couldn't help but to think of how cold and lonely it must be down there. But what was I thinking? Brian wouldn't know. After all, in my heart I knew that this was only temporary, he was just asleep in death. I knew that there was going to be a better life for all of us one day. But I wondered when?

We were going to take the train back home, but to my surprise Chief De Marco showed up as we were leaving. There was a nice-looking dark haired young lady standing beside him. He walked up to me and introduced her as his daughter Rebecca.

"Bailey, I know that I am not supposed to get personally involved in my cases, but like I told you before, there's just something about you. It's like my heart bleeds for you."

Rebecca walked up to me and gave me a hug. She must have been about my age and I believe we were about the same height and weight.

"Bailey, I want you to know that Dad won't rest until he brings this case to a close. Why don't you come on and let us take you out to the Sanka Coffee shop downtown. I think you probably could use a strong cup about now. We'll drop you off at your place afterwards, so don't worry about having to take the train home in all of this bitterly cold weather," she said as she looked me in the eyes with her ocean blue colored eyes.

"Ok. I think I'd like that. Thank you."

I thanked Janice and the others for coming and told her that I would call her later.

I normally didn't hang with strangers, but for some reason, this felt too genuine to be unreal. By this time Bae George had fallen asleep so I had to carry her everywhere we went.

I had a strange feeling that I was being made a part of someone's family, and it was beginning to feel good…

Mental State of Mind

For several weeks after Brian's murder I tried to maintain my sanity. I had given up my night job because if I hadn't been working that job to begin with, Brian would still be alive. This whole catastrophe is my fault. What kind of mother am I? Obviously not a good one or else my son would still be alive. Why didn't I ask Janice to check in on them? I bet I'll probably be questioning myself for the rest of my life.

I had been going back and forth to my general practitioner, Doctor James Stewart, for help with my pain. One day he told me that he could no longer help me. My mental state of mind was out of his range of expertise. He then referred me to a psychiatrist. A psychiatrist? Was I crazy? I didn't think so. I just couldn't sleep at night and felt extremely depressed from time to time. After all, I've been through a lot in my life.

My insurance authorized only two sessions with the psychiatrist, Doctor Joan Wilson. She is a tall, slender pretty blonde who wears a lot of gold and wore the finest suits I had ever seen. She didn't come across as being a friendly person, just a serious one. I guess professional is the word. During my visits with Doctor Wilson, we sat and talked about the things that happened in my life that caused my depression. She would counsel me, prescribe a couple of medications, including tranquilizers, and would call it a day. I figured okay, she's the doctor so she must know what she was doing. So I went and had the prescriptions filled…

Even though I began having weird side effects from the various medications, I continued taking them because the psychiatrist told me this was the only way that I was going to get better.

I wanted to get better but inside my head the medications felt like they were clashing against each other. I started having delusions of carrying on conversations with Brian and George. These delusions were so real that I frequently woke up yelling and screaming. And I was always drenched with sweat.

There were other times when I would see bugs crawling everywhere! I was terrified. This was so surreal! I am afraid of bugs, especially roaches. Sometimes while I slept I scratched my skin so vigorously that I drew blood. Plenty of times I woke up to see myself covered in blood.

I incessantly called Doctor Wilson but only got as far as her secretary. She always told me that Doctor Wilson was in with a patient and that she would call me back later. I never spoke with her so I had to assume that maybe she called back when I wasn't home.

My hallucinations were so bad that it got to the point where I was afraid to sleep at night. Because the tranquilizers always made me drowsy, it was always a constant battle to stay awake. This caused me to lose my job because I couldn't function. I felt helpless. I couldn't pick myself up out of this addictive condition. I was afraid to stop taking the medications because I honestly believed that they would eventually make me feel better.

Out of desperation I called Doctor Wilson again. This time she answered her line. I tried to explain my dilemma to her but she immediately cut me off and said, "Bailey, I am sure you're okay. You need to stop making a big deal out of everything. You're acting like a hypochondriac!"

She caught me completely off guard so much so that I almost dropped the phone.

"Excuse…excuse me Doctor Wilson, I'm sorry that you feel that way but I think I really have a problem."

Goodness, what had I done to bring that on?

"Look, continue taking all of your medications, and when your insurance authorizes more visits then I'll take some time with you. Wait a minute," she said as she shuffled through some papers, "It looks like your insurance has expired or lapsed. Can you afford to pay my fee yourself?"

"No, I'm not working right now. I can't afford your rate."

"Well, now I really can't help you. Call me when you can get up the money."

Click! I was dumbfounded. What had just happened? What was that all about? I felt even more depressed because I still needed help and now that I no longer had insurance I couldn't get it. Now what?

The next couple of weeks, I was totally out of my mind. I felt like I was a zombie who was living outside of my body. Poor Bae George, she was thoroughly confused by my behavior. That made two of us. I began to feel inadequate as a mother. I had a hard time dealing with simple things, and Bae George was too young to help me. I started having crazy urges that made me feel like I should be with George and Brian. I felt lonely and sad and I just wanted us to be a family. All of us, together again.

One breezy evening in February, I swallowed a lot of my prescription pills, put some items in my purse and dressed Bae George. I dressed myself and made sure that I was wearing my favorite red boots that George had purchased for me years earlier. Then we headed out the door.

We walked down to the Smith and 9th Street train station and took trains up to Grand Central Station. George used to take me there on occasion and treat me to my favorite pizza, at Big Sal's Pizza Chateau.

He liked Grand Central Station because of a famous scene in the *Untouchables* television series. Even though I never personally saw it and don't really know if it truly existed, he said that he loved the grandiose staircase that had been portrayed in the television series.

After Bae George and I arrived there and exited the train, I waited for most of the crowd to clear out before I lowered myself down onto the train tracks. Then I put my arms up to grab Bae George and lowered her down onto the tracks too.

"Hey lady! You crazy? Get back here!"

I was oblivious to everything.

"Nothing is going right for us. Everyone is against us," I babbled to myself.

I picked Bae George up and started walking down the tracks towards the path of the next arriving train.

"It's going to be okay, Bae George. Just close your eyes and before you know it, we will be with your grandmother, your dad, and your brother," I said under my breath.

"Don't worry, Brian, mommy's coming. Mommy and Bae George are coming to be with all of you. We can finally all be a family again. Something in my heart has been stabbing me, like icicles. I have to get rid of this pain."

Although I was oblivious to everything and everyone around me, I could hear and feel Bae George quietly sobbing against my chest.

"Mommy."

"Just a few more steps," I said as I finally saw the light in the tunnel from the oncoming train. I stared into the light.

"Mom, George, Brian, here we come!"

BAM! Total Darkness.

We made it…we finally made it…

Bae George

I opened my eyes to complete darkness. Why is it so quiet?

"Hello," I whispered.

No response. This time I spoke up a little louder, "Hello? Anybody there?"

At that moment, someone turned on a light. When I looked up to see who had turned it on, I gasped. It was a nurse.

"Where am I, and what am I doing here?"

The short, stumpy Caucasian nurse replied, "You are at the Manhattan Psychiatric Center. You tried to kill your daughter and yourself. It's sad that this poor child has a mother who would try to do something like this."

I tried to speak but she interjected and said, "Some women want children but can't have any. And it's a shame that people like you have them and try to get rid of them. How horrible!"

A doctor walked in at that precise moment.

"Mrs. Johnson, I'm afraid that I have some bad news for you," he said as he sat down by the hospital bed. After he sat down I noticed several people walking in behind him. I didn't have a good feeling about them.

"What's happening? What's going on? Where's my daughter Bae George?"

Once again I had that helpless feeling that made my mouth feel dry. It became difficult to speak.

The doctor said, "Save your breath. This is Rosa Hernandez from Child Protective Services."

This doctor who I have never seen before pointed to a humongous, short curly-headed Hispanic woman who was wearing a brown two-piece suit and a black pair of tacky-looking Buster Brown shoes. There was a look of doom written all over her sloppily made up face. Ugh, boy she needed a makeover badly. She did not crack a smile as she stood there with her worn-out, beat-up briefcase in one hand and a manila envelope in the other. My eyes grew wide when she started speaking.

"Mrs. Johnson, we have reason to believe that you are a danger to your child," she said with a strong Spanish accent.

What was she talking about? The room was spinning around and around until I thought I was going to throw up.

"What? What are you talking about?"

"Just be quiet and listen," she said sternly. "You were found walking on one of the train tracks in Grand Central Station. You had your daughter with you as you walked into the path of an oncoming train."

The effects of some of my medications were starting to wear off. I didn't have any idea what she was talking about.

"Fortunately for your daughter, an off-duty police officer managed to run into the tunnel and push you up against the wall away from the deadly 3rd rail and the oncoming train. The force from the push knocked you and your daughter unconscious. He held you there until the train passed. Your daughter is doing fine and of course you are fine too. Otherwise we would not be here."

"What are you saying?" I retorted. "Are you insinuating that I tried to kill myself and my daughter Bae George? I would never try to kill us! The thought never ever crossed my mind. I love my daughter too much!"

"How could you deny it? The facts speak for themselves! Look I don't know what kind of drugs you're on," Rosa Hernandez replied, "but that child does not deserve an addict for a mother."

"Addict? I'm no addict. My psychiatrist has me on so many different medications that sometimes I can't even remember what happens from one day to the next. That doesn't make me an addict. What gives you the right to label me?"

"Uh-huh, yep, sure, blame your drug addiction on someone else. It's always someone else's fault. So let me understand what I am hearing.

You are saying that your doctor forcibly put the drugs down your throat which caused you to become addicted, right?"

I hate it when people try to put words in my mouth. Everyone was staring at me while they shook their head in agreement with her.

"But…"

"Enough of this nonsense," Rosa Hernandez continued, "the bottom line is we reviewed your case and believe that it is in the best interest of the child if she was immediately removed from your care, or should I say, lack of care. Given the circumstances Bae George was immediately removed from your care and temporarily placed in a foster home. She is now with someone who can love and care for her the way a child should be taken care of. I assume that there isn't a father in the picture?"

"Well, no but, well yes but he's dead."

I want to die. I love Bae George with all my heart and would never intentionally try to harm her or myself in any way. My mind is getting clearer more and more every minute.

Oh God, please help me, I prayed silently to myself. Please don't let them take Bae George away from me.

I grabbed Ms. Hernandez's sleeve and started begging, "Please, please don't take my baby away from me. She's all I have in this world. I lost my mom, my husband and my son, and I don't know what I would do if I lost Bae George too. Please, I beg you, I'll get help, I'll do anything you want me to do but please don't take my baby away."

I started crying, but no one was hearing me. Some of the faces in the room started looking distorted and I started seeing double.

Ms. Hernandez jerked her arm back violently and said, "I'm sorry but it's over. It's a done deal and there is nothing that can be done about it. It's just as well that there isn't a father in the picture because the arrangements have already been made."

I knew I had lost, but I didn't want to relent.

"Can I at least see her one last time?"

"No." She coldly answered me.

"Why? Who is she with? Will I at least be able to keep in touch with her until I get well enough to get her back?"

"No, there probably won't be any opportunity for that any time soon. The doctor here signed the papers so that you will be confined and treated for mental illness at the Belle-Brooklyn Sanatorium. That is why these guys in the white jackets are standing behind me. They are taking you away immediately. Only the psychiatrist who is assigned to you there can sign to have you released."

One of the nurses jumped in with a snicker, "And you know that will never happen. She is definitely too far gone."

How dare these people stand here and judge me? I guess I have no choice but to believe that something happened if they are all saying so. They couldn't all be wrong. But I wish I could remember what happened. I am convinced that the medications have my mind all screwed up.

I know that I am not in the best frame of mind, but when I needed help not one professional was even willing to try…

The Clandestine Trip

W hen I arrived at the Belle-Brooklyn Sanatorium there was another van waiting there.

The driver, who is a pot-bellied Caucasian man said, "Good, it's about time you guys got here."

"What's going on?" I asked as the guys in the white jackets started pulling me out of the van and ushering me into the other van.

"Get in the van crazy woman," the driver said as he shoved me into the van.

"Where are you taking me? I have a right to know!"

The doors automatically locked and the van sped away. I looked around and noticed that there were several others in the van with me. Oh my God! What am I doing here? These people are crazy! One was talking to himself and another was counting the number of seats in the van. He must have had a compulsive disorder because he counted the seats over and over again. Front to back, and then back to front. He was getting on my nerves.

I thought I saw a woman who didn't look crazy but when I started speaking to her she went off on me. She started yelling out bible verses and telling me she was an angel. I slowly moved away from her.

"Hey driver! Where are you taking us?" I asked.

He looked up into the rearview mirror and said, "They told me that all of you were crazy. You sound sane to me."

"I am sane! This is some kind of trick so that they could take my daughter away from me. Can you help me?" I inquired.

He put a cigar in his mouth, lit it and started talking with it clinched in his teeth.

"Sorry sweetheart, I can't help you. I'm just the driver, I ain't got no authority at all. I wish I did 'cause I don't think you're crazy like the rest of them."

"Thanks, but I wish that the doctors felt the same way."

He continued, "In answer to your question, I was told that you all are going to be a part of an experiment. The sister to Belle-Brooklyn Sanatorium called Belle-Jax Sanatorium is located in Jacksonville Florida. I have to take all of you to the airport. There's a special charter plane waiting there. This whole experiment thing is supposed to be a big secret."

"Why would it be a big secret?"

"The way this asylum operates, I ain't a bit surprised. I've seen so many underhanded things take place that if the public only knew about it, this place would be shut down forever. But I need this job. I got six kids so I ain't saying nothing. I just do what they tell me to do. If you are indeed sane, I feel sorry for you 'cause you're in for quite a ride."

He got distracted for a second then said, "Oh here we are. There's the plane over there."

"Please sir, please help me?"

"I wish I could but I have too many mouths to feed. I don't make a lot but my family depends on me."

He stopped the van and told everyone to get out and get into the plane. When I walked passed him, I continued pleading with him. The end result was the same. I boarded the plane with all of the rest of the insane people. I was so afraid because I knew I didn't belong with them. I just needed a little help, but they needed a lot of help!

Belle-Jax Sanatorium

It was a dark bleak night in February when the plane landed at the Jacksonville International Airport. We were escorted down the stairs into the Belle-Jax van that was situated behind the airport. It was almost like the whole scene was clandestine.

I was not familiar with Jacksonville at all, but I kept my eyes open for any outstanding landmarks because I was already thinking about planning an escape. We soon arrived at the asylum. The darkness made it hard to see the street sign so I had no idea what it read. My hopes are high that one day soon I will be out of here and with my little girl again.

Oh Bae George, I sure miss you. I hope you know that mommy loves you dearly. It is driving me crazy to know you are out there with strangers. I couldn't help wondering how something like this could happen. I love my baby and I know in my heart that there isn't anyone out there who could take better care of her than I can.

I found out that all of us were going to be a part of this experiment. A couple of them were in strait jackets from the first moment that I got into the van with them. Since I wasn't acting violent at the time I was able to escape the strait jacket.

Each of us was put into our own little hole as I call it. The room was equipped with bars, which make it look like a prison cell. I looked around and saw a bed with a stiff mattress on it, a sink and a pewter toilet. I quickly found out that the doctors and nurses on the other side of the door controlled the lights. I had control over nothing. I was told when to eat, drink and sleep.

I was petrified that first night. The best thing I could think to do was to pray. I always remembered when there didn't seem to be anyone there for you, there is always God. I know he would never leave me stranded. Oh God, what did I do to deserve this treatment? I am so scared and all alone here with these crazy people. I am only off the wall because of the medications and my body's reactions to them. I'm sane enough to realize that. Why aren't the doctors sane enough to realize that too? Please help me and protect me, please…

After I prayed to God, I curled up in a ball and tried to fall asleep. It took a while because the mattress was so uncomfortable and the room was pitch black.

I was awakened the next morning by the sound of a key turning in the lock. When the nurse walked in, I could hear others out in the hallway yelling, screaming and moaning. That was scary. I wondered what that was all about, so I asked the nurse.

"Nurse, what's wrong with those people out there?" I inquired.

She retorted, "Never you mind, you will find out soon enough. Here take this medicine."

"What is it?"

"Just take it. You don't want me to shove it down your throat, do you?"

I thought goodness, what's up with that? This woman was much bigger than I was and I had no doubt she would do it. So I sat up, grabbed the pills and swallowed them with water. She stood there to make sure I swallowed them.

"Open your mouth," the nurse said.

I opened it to reveal that nothing was left unswallowed.

The Experiments

After what seemed like days, I woke up with an extremely intense headache. The bright lights shining in my face didn't help any. I tried to shield my eyes so I could see what was going on but to my annoyance I realized my arms were strapped beside me.

I tried to wiggle but my whole body was tightly restrained. Even my head was strapped to whatever this contraption was that I was hooked up to.

"It's about time you woke up."

A gruff looking Caucasian man stood over my face and pulled my eyelids back to check my pupils. I was still disoriented and overwhelmed by my whole crazy ordeal.

"What are you doing to me, and who are you?"

"Relax, I'm Doctor Scott. We are going to do a little experiment."

"Experiment? You don't have a right to experiment on me without my consent!"

"Listen, you're in my hospital and I am in charge here. What happens here is my business. And since you are confined here under my control, I don't need permission from you or from anybody else for that matter," he said matter-of-factly.

Judging by the way he looked and by what he was saying, I knew I was dealing with a monster. So I tried to appeal to his human side in hopes that he hopefully had one.

"Please doctor, don't hurt me. I'll do anything you say."

"Don't worry, you will not even feel a thing."

He lied…

When I woke up, I was in a daze. I couldn't remember all of the details of this treatment. But I did remember that whatever they did to me was excruciating. The pain was unbelievable and unbearable.

I have never felt that kind of pain in my whole life. I started whimpering like a baby and began to feel frightened again.

I tried to get out of bed but then realized that I couldn't get up on my feet, which caused me to fall to the floor.

It's a really weird feeling. It's as if I can't remember how to stand up or walk. I managed to pull myself back up onto the bed but this took a lot of strength and effort.

My head is killing me. I wonder how many procedures were performed? And why, why me? How do you just pick a person to torture like this? I'm not an animal. As a matter of fact, I wouldn't even want any animal going through this horror…

I believe I endured this pain for several months before I was clear enough to decide to plan my escape. I thought the experiments would have stopped by now or else I probably would have tried planning earlier.

After a while the asylum started allowing us to eat in the small cafeteria instead of eating in our rooms like solitary criminals. The tables in the cafeteria are so filthy and the eating utensils didn't appear to be that clean either. This didn't make any sense because these were plastic! They made sure we didn't have the real thing so that we couldn't hurt ourselves, someone else or even try to use it to escape. But at least this gave me a chance to be around others, no matter how crazy they were.

The workers were sane, so every chance I got, I eyed them to see if they had a daily routine that would help me with my escape plan.

While sitting at one of the tables one afternoon, I overheard the workers talking about a couple of patients who didn't survive one of the experiments. This one worker always seemed to love gossiping and on days that I am not heavily medicated, I can remember all that's spoken.

This short, young, skinny black worker was loud and tried to be heard all of the time. She was so loud that you couldn't help noticing her.

During one of their breaks, the three of them sat down at the table adjacent to mine and I pretended to be engrossed in the food on my plate. I didn't want them to know I was listening to their every word.

The skinny girl, whose name is Sheila, spoke first.

"Girl, did you hear about those two patients who died last night?"

"Nah, tell us about it," Dawn said.

"Well apparently Dr. Scott administered too many experiments on Miss Ellie and Mr. Friedman and they died before it was all over," Sheila said.

"No way."

"Yes way. I wonder how he's gonna get out of this screw up. He'll probably lie his way out of it like he did last time."

The third girl sat in silence while she listened to the others and kept an eye out for any signs of a manager coming in through the cafeteria doors.

While they were talking, I peered around to see what else was going on in the room. There were a handful of patients who were noticeably out of it. They acted like zombies.

Over to my left I watched a bus boy clean off some tables. Then he walked back and forth to the kitchen area carrying a trash bag. I started thinking, I wonder what time the trash is taken out and by whom? What is their process? Does a truck come by to pick it up? Or is it taken to the nearest dumpster?

Sheila's voice cut back into my thoughts.

"It's a shame. One of the families involved in his last mess up, or murder as I call it, was told that their relative died as a result of an acute case of the flu. And Mrs. Brown's family was told she died because of a heart attack. That woman was only thirty-five years old! Heart attack my eye!!"

"Yeah, I know a heart attack is possible at practically any age but she was a very young and healthy woman. Crazy maybe, but not sick," Dawn said.

The third girl decided to join in the conversation, "Yep, but I wonder why the families didn't question the death. To have a healthy person die just like that in a matter of weeks looks pretty suspicious to me. If I really loved that relative I would question that."

"Yeah, but you have to remember that most of these people's relatives wrote them off because they were mentally incompetent. And you know they never had any visitors. So they were at the doctor's mercy," Sheila said.

"Yeah, that's too bad. I hope that never happens to me. Shoot, to be written off like that is really sad," Dawn said.

Everyday when I go to the cafeteria, I keep watch on the workers' routines. The girls gossiped so much it was obvious that we were not being watched. There was usually around fifteen of us either eating or watching television and they never bothered us.

The television room is a small room off to the side of the cafeteria. Patients usually are allowed to walk from one room to the other. We just were not allowed to bring food from the cafeteria into the television room.

Everything was usually all right as long as someone didn't have one of his or her episodes. When this happened the place was chaotic.

But now that I think about it this kind of scene would provide a perfect time to try my escape.

There is this woman, Ella, who is a big boned black woman. I know she is off her rocker but somehow she manages to draw attention to herself at least once a week or two. For some reason, Saturday seems to be that day. I guess for one thing she loves the attention and for another there aren't as many workers watching us since it's the weekend. She seems to thrive on being able to overpower the few saps that are unfortunate enough to have to work during the weekends.

I think I have an idea of a way that I can get out of here. I've watched the bus boy for months now and I know where he gets the garbage bags to put the trash in. I heard him tell one of the new trainees to collect the garbage bags daily and pile them in the back of the old red pick up truck behind the kitchen door. Then on Saturday late afternoon, he is supposed to drive the pickup down the road to the dumpster.

My chance finally came weeks later.

The Escape

It is now the last Saturday in March 1986, and I am sitting in the cafeteria waiting for Ella to have her usual tantrum. I looked over at Dawn and the other two girls to see them in their usual huddle. I managed to lift one of the garbage bags from the new trainee's back pocket while he was cleaning my table. His pants were so baggy and loose that he didn't feel a thing.

I looked at the clock on the wall. It is seven in the evening and time for Ella to make her grand entrance.

She didn't disappoint me. Exactly ten minutes after arriving in the cafeteria she started having her fits. When the nurse's aides and the other workers ran over to restrain her I made my move.

I cautiously headed to the cafeteria door and looked for the truck. It was parallel to the door and was already packed with garbage to go.

No one was in the driver's seat yet, which was good for me. So I got up in the middle of the other garbage bags, opened my bag and positioned myself in it.

I was excited so I dressed for the occasion. Well, the only difference in my attire this day was the fact that I was wearing my favorite red go-go boots. We are supposed to only wear slippers but this day no one noticed because I wore a long white bedroom gown that reached down to the floor. The carpet concealed the sound of my heels. And when I sat at the table, I sat in a yoga position thereby hiding my boots under my gown.

I sat still in the bag and poked a small hole in it so that I could breathe. I once again sat in the yoga position to fold my legs to keep my boots from puncturing a hole in the bag.

Boy that garbage sure stinks! I thought to myself. But it doesn't matter, I will be out of here and reunited with Bae George soon.

Don't worry Bae George, mommy's coming. Just hold on, I'm coming.

I guess Ella's episode was over, because about fifteen minutes later, the truck started moving. It was heading to the dump, which I heard was in an open field a couple of miles down the road.

I started shivering because it's cold out today. The ride was bumpy but I had to keep reminding myself that my escape is worth it. There was no turning back now or ever.

The stench of the garbage was almost overwhelming, but I didn't have to deal with it for too long because the truck stopped after about ten minutes.

I heard a truck door slam shut and then two guys started talking. I peeked my head up out of the bag a little and saw that they were standing on the passenger's side of the truck. Then the two guys walked off a little, lit what looked like cigarettes and popped open two cans of beer.

I didn't get a good look at either of them because I was too busy jumping off of the driver's side of the truck.

I ran over to the ditch on the side of the road, and put my head down so as not to be seen. It was so cold as I laid down shivering in the garbage bag.

Every now and then I peeked up to see why the truck was still there. I figured out that the driver was probably drunk by now and was not in any hurry to get back to work. He'll probably lie about what took him so long, if anyone noticed.

About a half hour later, he finally got into the truck, made a U turn and drove off. The other guy too got in his truck and drove off.

So there I was, cold, and alone in the darkness…

Seek Shelter

After the coast was clear, I got up out of the ditch and started walking in the opposite direction of the asylum. I made sure that I stayed close to the side of the road to avoid being detected. I walked up to the nearest sign, which read Talleyrand Avenue. I have never been to Jacksonville, so I was not familiar with the areas around here. I knew that one day I was going to visit Deja and see the city of Jacksonville, but goodness not like this!

Over to the right side of the road was a river or some body of water, so when I came up to the next road, 8th street, I turned left. As I walked, I noticed how decrepit the houses looked. I must be in the old or Historic section of town. There were raggedy looking stray dogs walking around scrounging for food and trash was all in the streets. Filthy!

At this time of year it was too cold for anyone to be standing outside on the stoop, or in their case, the porch. Which was good for me because I looked like a mess. Here I am out here in a long white cotton nightgown wearing red boots. Boy that is really smart! I stand out like a sore thumb.

My legs are starting to hurt from all of this walking. Heels weren't made for all of this walking! I walked up to an old abandoned house that I hoped was empty. When I reached it and peeked in, I saw that the front room was empty. Many of the windows were boarded up which helped to shield me a little from the cold.

I sat over in a corner, petrified out of my wits. What in the world is happening to me? How did all of this crazy stuff happen? This whole thing is unreal. I wish it was just a dream, but because of my luck, or lack of, this is real.

I started getting hungry and remembered that I had stuffed my pockets with food. The chicken was so greasy that the grease seeped through the pockets in my gown. My corn bread was now mainly crumbs. But I ate it all. I also didn't want to leave any crumbs around just in case there were some rodents lurking around here too. They weren't getting dinner invitations from me!

As I sat in the dark on my garbage bag munching hungrily on my food, I started recollecting events in my life. I miss Bae George and everyone else so badly. My family has fallen apart.

Just then Deja popped into my mind. I wonder where she lives and what she's doing right now? All I can recall about where she lives is something about living downtown in a new high-rise apartment building. I tried searching my mind to see if I could remember anything else she said about where her place was located. I pondered that thought for a while until things started coming together in my head. I remembered Deja saying something about the Jacksonville Landing and downtown Jacksonville.

I wonder how far I am from downtown. I'll have to check that out early in the morning because I am sure the people from the asylum must be out looking for me…

Butchie

The next morning I woke up to the sound of something moving. After my eyes adjusted to the darkness, I looked over to my right and saw what looked like a big black rat scurrying around. I covered my mouth to keep from screaming out loud. I guess it's time for me to leave! I hope there aren't any more rodents in my path.

I slowly got up so as not to disturb him, looked out the front of the house and walked out.

It must have been really early because no one was out and about yet.

One of the first things I have to do is find something to cover my gown. I continued walking down 8th street passed Thelma and Brackland Streets when something on a nearby porch caught my eye.

The house was lime green and had several large windows facing the street. There was also a big wooden porch in the front of the house. I slowly crept onto the porch and spotted a brown windbreaker. I put it on and found it to be a little big, but it'll do. I lifted my gown up around my waist and tucked it into my underwear to make it look more like a dress.

The weather was brisk which caused me to walk swiftly. I was looking for at least one person who could give me directions to Deja's apartment building.

I stopped at a seven eleven store near Walnut street. Even though it seemed to be early, the lights were on. I attempted to push the door open but it was locked. I peeked in and saw a short, skinny black man with a receding hairline, mopping the floor. I knocked on the glass door and he motioned that he's closed. I tried communicating with my hands to show him I needed to use the phone. He walked over to the door and looked out to see if I had anyone else with me. He opened it to let me in, and then closed and locked the door behind me.

"Thank you," I stuttered because I was shivering so badly.

"Girl, what ya doing out in the cold this early in the morning?" The storekeeper asked.

"Please sir, I need to use the phone."

He pointed to the phone behind the counter. I walked over and dialed information to get Deja's number or big Miles' number but neither was listed. I wonder why she didn't list her number? This is upsetting.

"What's wrong girl? You look like you lost your best friend."

"I think I did. I'm from out of town and I am trying to get in touch with my best friend. I don't have her number but I know that she lives in some new high-rise apartment building somewhere downtown. Have you heard of any new apartment buildings downtown?"

"Yep. If I am correct they built some about six months to a year ago. I think they are called The River Walk Suites."

He paused and scratched his head then said, "Wait a minute, there's also the Landing Estates Apartments. But about two weeks ago I heard there was a problem with one of those buildings. But I don't know which one it was or what happened. Do you want a ride down there? Downtown is not too far from here."

"Well sir– "

"They call me Butchie," he said.

"Ok Butchie, I would appreciate it. I hope this doesn't interfere with your work here."

"Shucks girl, I own this place. I can shut down at any time. Besides I don't open for a couple more hours. I just couldn't sleep so I figured I would come in early and get things in order. Stay right there, I will be right back," Butchie said.

I had no choice but to wait and hope that he wasn't a pervert. I knew I was kind of at his mercy.

Butchie returned out of the back room with his coat on and car keys in hand.

"Hey girl, what's your name?"

"Bailey."

"Ok, here girl, take this sweater so you don't freeze to death," he said as he handed me a black wool sweater from behind the counter.

I had to laugh to myself because he requested my name, and then called me girl anyway. That was cute.

"This used to belong to my wife. God rest her soul."

I didn't feel that it was my place to inquire about her so I didn't.

"Hey girl, you look hungry. Go over there and grab some snacks. And have a cup of coffee too. I brewed a fresh pot."

I walked over to the rack and grabbed some chips and some coffee cakes. I also poured a large cup of black coffee. I took one swallow and ah, this is just what I needed.

We walked outside to his old grey Cadillac. I don't know what year his car was but it looked like it was as old as he was. Parts of the car were falling off.

He was quite the gentleman as he opened the door on my side first. Despite how old this car was, the inside was neat and spotless.

You could tell that this car was his baby. After he sat down in the car and started the engine, he said, "Here, let me put some heat on to keep you warm. It's gonna take a few minutes though."

"Thanks."

"No problem girl."

He pulled the car away from the curb and drove us down this street called Main Street. How original I thought. I noticed there were an awful lot of pawnshops and small car lots along the blocks. We rode passed a restaurant called Popeye's chicken. I had never heard of that restaurant. We didn't have a Popeye's chicken up north.

"What kind of restaurant is that? Is it like Kentucky Fried Chicken?" I asked as I pointed to the restaurant.

"Well it's on a different level. Kentucky Fried Chicken costs more and has a different flavor than Popeye's. They're both good. It just depends on what you have a taste for. You should try it while you're here in town."

"I'll have to see."

"I know it's none of my business but what's going on with you girl? You appear out of nowhere, on foot in the freezing cold, wearing what looks like pajamas. Don't you know you can catch a death of cold?" Butchie asked.

I shook my head yes. I didn't really want him to get suspicious in case the asylum should happen to be in his neighborhood inquiring about me. I told him I would stay out of the weather once I got to Deja's place.

It didn't take long to reach downtown.

"Well here we are girl," he said as he pulled up along side the curb near a tall building.

I suddenly thought of something. It just occurred to me that I gave him my real name. Stupid! That will definitely make it easy for him to turn me in if the asylum questioned him about me. I have to hope that since he still called me girl he must have forgotten my name, or didn't pay attention enough to remember it. But what are the chances? My name is not a common name. Oh well, I can't dwell on that.

"Thank you."

"Do you want me to wait for you just in case?"

"No thank you. I'll be ok."

"Are you sure?"

"Yes, I'm sure."

"Ok girl, take care," he said as he took my little hands in his big hands.

When he let go I felt something in the palm of my hand. I looked down and saw dollar bills.

With a twinkle in his eyes he said, "Your secret's safe with me. If you need me, you know where my store is. If I am not there, someone will get a message to me. Take care of yourself Bailey."

He smiled and drove off.

I stood there dumbfounded for a second. So he knew my name the whole time. And for him to say my secret is safe with him tells me that he knew more about my situation then he was letting on. Had he helped other people who might have escaped from the asylum?

The High-Rise
Apartment Building

After Butchie drove off, I looked up at the sign on the building, which read, The River Walk Suites. It is an impressive looking building. The outside was made of some type of greystone, and when I walked inside I looked around in awe of the shiny marble floors, the gigantic chandelier and the two winding staircases.

I walked up to the security guard's desk, and was greeted with a look of disgust by the rent a cop security guard.

"We don't let vagrants in here," the security guard said.

"Excuse me?"

He stepped from behind the desk, took me by the arm and said, "Get out, we don't allow your kind in here."

I tried to shrug him off me.

"I am not a vagrant, and get your hands off me!"

"What do you want? Money? A place to sleep?" he asked snidely.

"No sir, I am looking for my sister, I believe she lives in this building."

He calmed down a little and walked back behind the desk and said, "Ma'am, I am so sorry. I thought you were one of those homeless people trying to find a warm place to stay."

"You shouldn't prejudge someone because of how they look. Anyway, I am looking for Kahadeja Cummings or Miles Lee."

He thumbed through the resident log, and shook his head.

"No, they are not on this list."

"But they gotta be on this list, they moved here about six months ago or so."

"Nope, they aren't here."

"I don't believe it. Could you perhaps look for Kahadeja Lee or Deja Cummings or Deja Lee, please?"

He looked again, this time he took his time.

"No, I'm sorry ma'am. She is not on this list. None of those names are on the list. Is it possible that she lives in a different building?"

"I guess that's possible. She moved into a new high-rise apartment building somewhere downtown. I don't remember the name of the place."

"Well in the past year there have only been two new high-rise apartments built in the downtown area. Maybe she stayed at the other apartments. Those were called the Landing Estates Apartments."

"Where are those apartments?" I asked full of hope.

"Well, like I said, they *were* called the Landing Estates Apartments, they used to be on Water Street."

"What do you mean by used to be?"

"There was a fire there about two weeks ago. I don't know all of the specifics, but the news said that an electrical spark caused it. Apparently the building was constructed too quickly, and some inspections kind of slipped through the cracks. You know what I mean? Anyway, there are several lawsuits pending against this developer for negligence." The security guard volunteered.

"But, but what about the people who were living there? How can I find out if my sister is okay?"

"I don't know what to tell you since the whole building burned down to the ground, there isn't anywhere for them to post any information about the tenants. Why don't you try calling the news or something? They should have some kind of information, or maybe they can point you in the right direction."

"Oh that's just great. I hope my sister and her family are all right."

"The odds are that they survived. Only about five people died in that fire," he said matter-of-factly.

"Only about five people? Goodness! It might seem like only five people to you but they belonged to somebody! What a shame to die a horrible death like that! To be burned to death! Oh my God, I hope my sister isn't among those five," I replied.

I could tell that he felt bad about his comment, because he tried to redeem himself when he said, "I'm sure your sister is okay. I'm sure that a lot of people weren't at home at the time. She probably was one of them."

"I don't know what to do. My grandparents died in a fire years ago and I don't think I could handle it if this happened to my sister too. Do you have the number to a news station?"

He pulled out a phone book, thumbed through it and said, "Let me see, here's a number to the Channel 6 Chaos News. I would let you use this phone but the station is closed this early. Here I'll put it on this paper, you can take it with you."

"Thanks." I took it and stood there and thought, now what? What am I going to do? Where will I go? Where's Deja?

I started feeling depressed, and realized I didn't have my medication. The medication that the doctors at the asylum had me taking seemed to have worked better than the meds my psychiatrist had put me on. Well, maybe not at first, but towards the end of my stay.

I am so afraid that I will end up unbalanced again. The doctors told me that I had a chemical imbalance that required treatment so that it could be kept under control. Sometimes when I didn't take my medication I started to feel weird side effects, like I am outside of my body looking in and wondering what is going on with me!

I walked out of the building wondering what's my next step? I know I don't want to go back to that asylum because I want to be with my baby.

It was still dark outside when I started walking aimlessly down Forsyth Street. I have no idea where I am going or what I am going to do. I wish I had family I could call. But then again, their conscience might induce them to turn me in.

A second later I heard a voice over my left shoulder.

"Psss, hey girl. You looking fine."

When I turned around all I saw were stars…

The Disguise

"Ohhh," I said while I held the back of my head. I felt a big knot forming.

I looked around to see that I was on my back in some alley. I was surrounded by buildings, and there was a green dumpster on the corner.

I stood up and stumbled around for a few minutes, until I saw a man sitting with his back to one of the buildings. He was unshaven and acted as if he was inebriated. He also was singing to himself. I left him alone and started stumbling towards a well lit entryway and sat down for a little while.

What happened? I wondered. Why would someone hit me? I checked my pockets and oh no, the dollars Butchie gave me were gone! That's just great! Bad enough I am out here like this, but it's worse without money in my pocket.

I'm starting to get hungry. Where can I get food at this hour? Whatever hour it is. I hate not having a watch! I am totally at a lost for time. I know some cities have places like a soup kitchen where you can go to get a free meal. I hope Jacksonville, as big as it is, has some soup kitchens.

Oh I just had a thought. If Jacksonville has soup kitchens, I can't go there looking like this. I have to somehow disguise myself just in case the people at the asylum are still looking for me.

I got up and continued down the alley. As luck would have it I came upon a store that appeared to have used items outside in black garbage bags and in some trash cans. I'm not too keen on digging through trash or even wearing other people's clothes but I am desperate. I refuse to go back to the asylum. I have to get back to my Bae George.

I started pulling things out until I came across a brand new short black wig that was still in the original box. There were other new items too like hats and old style dresses. So I grabbed a brown hat and a green cotton dress. It was the longest dress I could find. I looked around and saw that nobody was watching me. Then I put the green cotton dress on over my clothes. So there, now I look a little on the plump side. I shoved my hair under the wig and put the brown hat on over it. There, that's better. I know I look silly but who cares? It's a disguise and the best one that I could find at the moment.

I looked down, and thought, oh boy a green dress and red go go boots! Nuts! Oh well, I have to do what I have to do. Besides, the asylum will be looking for someone who is thin and with all of these clothes on, and with this wig on, they'll never know.

The Soup Kitchen

I got up and started walking. I don't know where I'm going but I hope I bump into someone who is going my way.

I walked from Ocean Street to Church Street. And up ahead I saw a bunch of people standing around in the dark. As I approached them I saw that they looked worse than I did.

I walked up to a halfway decent looking black man and said, "Excuse me sir, I am looking for a soup kitchen or a shelter."

"Well ma'am you've come to the right place. That's why we're all standing out here freezing," he said.

"What time do they open the doors?" I inquired.

"I don't have a watch but judging by the looks of this line, I'd say probably within the next fifteen minutes or so. Make sure you don't wander off this line, because you'll lose your spot. And around here people fight for spots. Once they fill up, they cut off the line, so watch your back," he said.

"Thanks for the advice. By the way, my name is Betha." I said but I didn't reach out to shake his extended hand. Lord knows where it's been. So I kept mine in my pockets.

"And I'm James," he said as he put his hands back in his pockets. He had sensed my apprehension.

I started shivering. Boy I hope they open these doors soon. I looked around and observed my surroundings. There were about twelve people in front of me and several more started lining up behind me. Some were women but the majority were men. Old and young, there were all kinds of people. With this get up I am wearing, I look older. So far so good with my disguise.

Finally after what seemed like forever, the doors opened and people started pushing. We were no longer standing in a single line. I pushed and shoved just like the rest of them. After all this is about survival.

Once inside I saw several tables with plastic chairs on one side of the room, and on the other side were tables that were set up with a display of food. The people standing behind the food had aprons on with the words "Welcome Friends" on it.

It sure smells good in here. There were bacon and egg sandwiches, hot grits, and different flavors of soups, juice, water and fruit. I took a tray, walked along the line, and requested a bacon and egg sandwich, juice and some grapes, and for some reason a bowl of grits. I had never eaten grits but wanted to know how they tasted.

I looked for an available seat at the far corner of the room and found one at a small table for four. After I sat down, James came over to sit down and two women sat down beside him. I could tell they were friends because they were involved in a deep conversation. I am a persnickety person and despite my circumstances I proceeded to pick the fat off the two pieces of bacon and put the bacon back into the sandwich. People probably thought I was crazy or hoity toity. But who cares what they think?

"You're new here. Where have you been hiding?" James said as he stuffed a piece of bread in his mouth.

I have to be careful and play my cards right.

"Well you know, it's just one of those things. You know, I woke up one morning and kinda found myself here." I hope that is evasive enough to end the conversation.

"Ok," he sighed, "you don't want to talk about yourself I take it, am I right?"

I shook my head then said, "What about you?"

I kept my eye on him because even though he appeared to be nice, I'm new to this environment and I don't want to get hurt.

"Well ma'am, I don't mind talking about myself. But my story is long and boring. Let me see, I used to have a wonderful life. Ha, isn't that the name of a movie? Anyway, I owned a business on the Southside of Jacksonville, had a pretty wife, kids, a big house and a bright red BMW. I had arrived!"

"When my business went belly up, the wife split with the kids and with all of our savings. I lost everything. I don't even know where my kids are. I ended up depressed and homeless and have been reduced to waiting for food like a criminal. They don't give welfare to guys like me, so I've been working odd and end jobs during the day, and at night I stay in a shelter."

"That's too bad," I said.

He hurriedly swallowed another bite and said, "It's not that bad, it could be worse. At least I have somewhere to lay my head at night and I get free meals. I'm saving my money because one day I will be back on track. And when I do get back on track, I'll search for my kids," James said.

"That was evil of her, and selfish too if I might add. How long have you been homeless?"

"Let me see, I'm thirty-eight now, so it's been about two years. My kids should be three and four now. You got kids?" James asked.

My eyes averted his because I didn't want him to see that I was tearing up.

"I'm sorry ma'am. I forgot." Then he changed the subject and said, "How about you stay at the shelter tonight? They have a temporary section for women. You could stay there a couple of nights to get yourself together. It's not too far from here."

"Ok, I might just do that, thanks."

The soup kitchen staff let us stay about an hour and then stated that they would see us at dinnertime.

I stood outside with James and said, "Dinnertime? What do people do during the day?"

"Most of us have a two bit job, some stay lined up out here, and others walk the streets and beg for money. Not everyone who comes here is sane, if you know what I mean."

"Yes I think I know."

"That's another reason why you have to be careful, they'll do anything for drug or alcohol money."

The Shelter

I decided to take James' advice and look for the shelter. I was told that the shelter, called The New Life Inn Shelter, was on State Street. Some people gave me directions that led me to the entrance of the shelter. I wasn't too crazy about the type of men who were hanging around the outside of the building but they didn't try to mess with me. I guess I looked too bad for any of them to even think about wanting to get with me. Good!

I walked into the building and spoke with a woman who ushered me into a private room.

"This is the men's facility. The women's facility is on McDuff. You can stay for about three nights but after that you will be transferred to the other facility," she said.

"Here they have a small section that is reserved for women. Follow me to the women's section, which is on the second floor," she continued.

She had to put in a special code in order to open the door. When she opened the door, I saw a young girl curled up in a ball, sleeping on a cot. She must have been no more than about nineteen or twenty.

The director, whose name is Daisy, said, "That's Janelli. She's also going to McDuff in a couple of days."

I glanced over at her. She was so young. I wondered what she was doing here.

On the other side of the room, there were three women who looked like they were trouble. I don't like to prejudge, but I just had that feeling.

Once I got settled, a couple of hours later Daisy took me down to their little cafeteria so that I could grab a bite to eat. After eating, Daisy gave me a small bag that contained necessary feminine products and other necessary items. She gave me clean linen, a blanket and a new nightgown that I could keep and also showed me where the bathroom and shower were located.

"Make yourself comfortable and if you need anything, just use the intercom on the wall. Don't worry about the guys downstairs, they can't get into this room without the code. And only a few of us know the code," Daisy said.

Daisy seemed to be so sweet. She's a petite black woman, with a shoulder length Jheri curl. She seems to have a good aura about her.

After she left, I sat on one of the cots near Janelli. Those other women occupied the other cots.

"Hey, that's my cot," one of them said.

I thought, oh crap, I don't need this.

"Hey, didn't you hear me?" she said as she started walking towards me.

She was scary looking and had a wry expression on her face. She's a big black woman, who looked like she was hardened by life. She had cornrows that were braided back from her face, a low forehead and was tall yet pudgy in shape. She looked like she had just been released from prison.

I was scared but didn't want her to know. Her two friends got up too and started walking towards me. Man, what can I do? I guess the best thing to do is to act crazy. So I stood up and braced myself.

"Yep I heard you. But this is my cot and I am not moving." At that moment Janelli woke up, got up and stood in the corner out of the way.

This big woman came up to me and caught me off guard with a push. I fell down onto the cot. I then jumped her at the waist. We rolled onto the floor. Her friends jumped on me from behind. I was punching her and trying to kick and punch them at the same time. I somehow managed to get all of them off of me and stood up and said, "You don't want to mess with me! I'll kill you!"

"Right, you couldn't kill a fly," the big woman said as she wiped sweat off of her face.

"You don't know me. I lost my mother, my husband, my daughter and my son was murdered. I have nothing to lose if I kill you. And trust me you don't want to mess with someone like me! Because I am crazy!" I yelled.

Then to drive home the point, I started walking around yelling out loud and making gestures. I opened my eyes really wide and yelled to the girls that I am *crazy*. And then I started making more crazy sounds. People who acted this way always scared me. So anytime I saw this behavior on the streets, I would cross the street or if I saw it on television, I would turn the channel.

The girls backed off. And poor Janelli was obviously frightened.

"You crazy woman, stay away from me!" yelled the big woman with a frightened look on her face.

I guess she figured that it was not worth it to mess with a crazy woman. She was not as tough as she thought she was. She was out of her league. Which honestly was true because I knew that I was not 100 percent stable after all that I have been through in my life.

After this altercation I sat down on the cot, put my head down on my pillow, relaxed and went to sleep. I was not afraid for my life because I knew that these girls had gotten the message.

The next day, a woman by the name of Reena came into the shelter. There was something about her that rubbed me the wrong way and for some reason I lunged at her. I think that maybe she reminded me of that nurse Wright. Or maybe it was my mind playing tricks on me.

A couple of days later they were moving us to the facility at McDuff, but I decided that I didn't want to go. I ended up on the streets again.

Life on the Streets

I spent a lot of time on the streets. Each year that I spent homeless, I went back and forth to the soup kitchen until it closed each summer. They were mainly open during the winter months and around the holidays.

At night I often huddled with others in an abandoned building. On occasion I had to fight for a warm spot, and keep a close eye on my little bit of possessions. The experience was horrible and the fact that I didn't have my medications made me feel crazy and on occasion act crazy. There were days when I would feel like I was outside my body looking in on myself. I also walked around downtown talking out loud to myself from time to time. I can't explain why but something inside me propelled me to act this way.

People always got out of my way whenever I walked into their path. I guess I can't blame them, I was kind of afraid of myself too, if that makes any sense.

I thought I saw that Reena girl again one summer. She was walking around Hemming Park or Plaza trying to get homeless people to come to her shelter. She was talking and handing out pamphlets. Boy she sure got herself together after she moved on from that New Life Inn Shelter.

I know she saw me walking around but didn't bother asking me if I wanted to go to her shelter. For the life of me I don't know why I didn't go at that time. At least I would have had clean clothes on my back and I would not have had to scrounge for food. After I found out that the soup kitchens were not a permanent fixture I was reduced to begging for food and money and eating leftovers out of garbage cans.

Yuck, that food was so disgusting! Every now and then I was able to get some untouched food that I found in a dumpster behind a fast food place. I guess this was food people had ordered, then returned because it was the wrong order. And the establishment threw it out, which of course was a good thing for me as long as I didn't have to fight with other homeless people to get to it.

I got so sick of being dirty and homeless that years later I somehow managed to get to one of those shelters that Reena had established. I really don't know why it took me so long to get to one. Maybe it was my pride, stupidity or my unstable mental state of mind.

Back into Society

Ｉt's now the winter of 1994. A couple of years ago, I started getting myself together at one of Reena's shelters called 'Help for the Homeless', on State Street.

It took a while, but the people at the shelter succeeded in helping me get myself together. I was taught a trade, proper interviewing etiquette, self-esteem, cleanliness, as well as other things that I needed to make the transition back into society. I was also screened for mental and physical health, after which I had several follow up meetings with a psychiatrist.

He helped me work out a lot of things in my life and in my mind. I am now able to see things a lot clearer.

The first thing on my mind now is to find Bae George. It's been years now and she should be about sixteen years old. I bet she is even more beautiful than before. I have so many questions, like how does she look, where is she at, who raised her?

The administrators at the shelter helped me find housing on Liberty Street, in the Ridgetown Apartments. Although these apartments were a little run down, and the area was not safe, I managed to keep to myself and stay out of trouble. The police were always on or near the premises so instead of looking at this as a negative, I saw this as a positive. There were times when I got home late from work and felt uncomfortable walking home from the bus stop, but then I would look up and see a police car and I would feel okay. I always said hello to the officers. Even though most of them were really aggressive, they had good reason to be. They didn't seem to prejudge all of the people who lived in my neighborhood, which was a good thing. They knew that a lot of us were living here because we were trying to get back on our feet. But of course, there are always bad apples in any bunch.

The administrators had also assisted me in finding employment in my field again, which was the banking field. I interviewed at several different places, and managed to get hired on to Barnett Bank as a keypunch operator.

It was slow going at first because I had not done this kind of work in years. But in no time I was meeting production like the others, and bringing in a regular paycheck.

Now that this part of my life is stable, it was time to look for Bae George…

The Search Begins

Istarted my search by calling the Manhattan Psychiatric Center. When I dialed information, I was told that it is now called the Center for Psychiatric Assistance.

"Hello, I need to speak with someone in your records department," I said.

"One moment." The operator replied as she put me through to records.

"Records, can I help you?" A voice on the other side inquired.

"Yes, my name is Bailey Johnson, and I was a patient there years ago when this was called the Manhattan Psychiatric Center. Social services took my daughter away from me and I need help finding her."

"I don't know if I can give any information over the phone. You might need to come in." The records clerk stated.

"Miss, you don't understand. I am calling from Florida. There is no way that I can come into the hospital to take care of this. Please, my daughter is missing. Listen, you have children don't you?"

"Well yes, I have a two-year-old son."

"How would you feel if someone took your two-year-old away from you? Wouldn't you try your hardest to search for him?" I tried to appeal to her heart.

"Well yes, but…"

"Then please help me. Please. What is your name?" I begged.

"Vanessa."

"Vanessa, please?"

"Ok I will see what I can do. It might not be much because a lot of the records mysteriously disappeared right before the Center for

Psychiatric Assistance took over. What is your daughter's name, the social worker's name, the doctor's name who treated you, and the year that this happened?" Vanessa asked.

I gave Vanessa all of the pertinent information, and then said, "I am calling long distance. Do you have a toll free number?"

"No, but I'll tell you what, I will research this and I'll call you back. When is a good time for you?"

"I get in from work during the week around 6 p.m. EST. Are you still at work then?"

"I'll stay late, and call you tomorrow. But I don't want you to get your hopes up high because for one, I should not be doing this over the phone, for two a lot of the older records are gone, and for three if anyone finds out about this, I will get fired."

"I promise I won't tell anyone. I just want my baby back," I said as I fought back my tears and gave her my home phone number.

"Bailey, expect my call tomorrow," Vanessa said.

"Vanessa, thank you very much, you are a blessing. Good-bye."

After I hung up the phone, I sat on my bed praying. I just have to find my baby. She is all that I have...

Vanessa's Call

After I arrived home from work the next day, I expectantly sat by the phone wishing it to ring. Finally!

"Hi Bailey? This is Vanessa."

"Hi Vanessa, do you have any good news for me, I hope?"

"Unfortunately for you I didn't find much. I will tell you what I did find out, but first I want to make absolutely sure that you are indeed her mother. You stated that they took Bae George away from you, and all of the dates and people involved panned out. But I need to know what, if anything, happened to you. Because only the real Bailey would know this and I would have no doubts as to who you are," Vanessa said.

"Ok that is only fair," I said as I proceeded to tell her what I went through and where I ended up.

"That's so sad. I am so sorry that you went through that. They sealed the records, but in sealing them, they managed to leave one little part out."

"What? What is it?"

"The records indicated that she was adopted by a bi-racial political family, who had no children of their own. And the man, who is black, was running for some kind of office, and needed a child to complete his family and his chances of winning. Even though there weren't any names given, this is a big boost to help in your search for Bae George."

"Wow, Vanessa, thank you for this information. This is a big help. Because when you think of it, how many bi-racial political families were there during that time, where the man was running for some kind of office? I will see what kind of research I can do down here in Florida. Do you know what avenues I should try to get information from New York?"

She gave me some ideas, and reminded me that it will be hard unless I were in New York doing this research. But I am a determined woman, and figured I would do what I could here in Florida.

"Vanessa, thank you again."

"I wish I could have been of more help. And if I ever get a chance to do a little research myself, I will let you know. It's hard to do much with a two-year-old, a full time job and college classes. And on top of all of this, I am a single parent because my kid's dad decided that he was too young to take care of a kid. Anyway, you take care. And Bailey, I know that I don't personally know you, but I want you to know that I do have a heart, and I do feel for you. Take care," Vanessa said.

"Vanessa, pray for me and my daughter. Good-bye."

Research

I called several of the major newspaper offices in New York City until I got someone on the line who was able to put their attitude away for a minute and answer some of my questions. I was told to go to my local library where I could pull reels of archived papers on microfiche. So I did just that.

I went to the main Jacksonville library downtown, and asked the information clerk for assistance. He directed me to the area that I needed, showed me how to do my research, and how to load and unload the film onto and off of the machine and how to print copies of what I wanted.

I went to the library everyday after work scanning through the archives for any information on this bi-racial political family. After a month, I was elated to finally find some information that I hope leads me to my Bae George.

I printed out the information, and went home to read and absorb it.

Around the time Bae George was taken from me, I found out that there were several people running for various different offices in the state of New York. The family that stood out from the rest was the Martin family. In their picture there was a little girl holding the wife's hand with her face turned slightly away from the camera. It looked like this was done intentionally. But I instantly knew who this little girl was.

The Martin family consisted of a tall handsome black man by the name of Johnny, his short slender Caucasian wife Jane, and their beautiful six-year-old black daughter June. In looking at the pictures,

I knew this was Bae George. Every mother knows her child. Besides, turning her face away from the camera didn't really hide her features. It was her as clear as day.

One of the articles that was printed stated that Johnny was running for a Senate position in the Manhattan district of New York. His chances were great because of his work ethics, his contacts and his credentials.

I was impressed with most of the articles about him and his family, including the one about his adopting this beautiful little girl. But was soon dismayed when I read on to find that it painted a sad story of her life. It stated that her mother was a drug user who beat and neglected her. The fact that he adopted her and took her away from this heinous situation really helped his appeal with the public. Rats, now it's going to be that much harder to try to contact her, I thought. Then I looked at an article dated months later, and my jaw and my heart dropped…

The Article

The article stated in big, bold letters, "DEAD. Johnny Martin, who was running for the state Senate and his wife Jane Martin of Manhattan, were found dead in their Manhattan apartment on Park Avenue at 9 p.m. on Saturday. Their housekeeper found their bloody lifeless bodies in the study, after she returned home from a trip to the supermarket. The little girl, June was found safe but crying and holding the kitchen phone. Apparently she had attempted to call for help." The smaller print stated that it appeared to be a murder. Later articles brought to light the fact that Jane caught Johnny cheating again after she stuck by him through previous infidelities. They got into a heated discussion about the other women, then a full-blown altercation, where there was yelling and items being thrown around. There was also evidence of a major struggle. The end result was when Jane ran into the study followed by Johnny, reached into the top desk drawer, grabbed the family pistol, and in the heat of the moment shot Johnny several times until he was dead. June had run into the room just in time to see Jane standing there crying with the pistol to her head. Next thing she knew, Jane was on the floor bleeding to death. June was taken into state custody, where she eventually was adopted out again to a less prominent family who moved from New York to Georgia. This case had been closed as a murder suicide.

Georgia

Oh my God! My baby went through all of this and just like that she was shipped off to the next family. I know she was only six at that time, but kids can be affected by disasters like these, especially if they don't have anyone to help them deal with it.

I wonder how she fared with her new family? Did she bounce back from this tragic point in her life? Did this family love and treat her well?

I started praying. I hope my baby survived and is alive and well. She deserves no less than a good life.

Now I have to redirect my research to the state of Georgia. I called most of the state agencies in Georgia and was either given the runaround or simply told that no information could be released due to privacy statutes.

I started saving my money so that I could take a trip to the Georgia state capitol, Atlanta. This would afford me the opportunity to explore other avenues that would hopefully help me find Bae George. This research was even harder because this adoptive family was not in the limelight.

On a whim, I decided to go to Atlanta's missing persons bureau to file a missing person's report.

Missing Persons Unit

I managed to take a couple of days off work and on a Monday, I rode the Greyhound Bus to downtown Atlanta. I stayed at a hotel on Peachtree Street. Later that day I went down to the main police station to their missing person's department.

I went into this dank, stuffy office and walked up to the counter. There were a couple of young girls behind the counter talking about things like the date they had last night.

I stood there annoyed then made the first move, since they didn't bother.

"Excuse me."

"Yes ma'am, what can I help you with?" One of them asked as she made her way over to the other side of the counter.

"I want to file a missing person's report," I said.

She reached under the desk, and handed me this clipboard with papers and a pen attached to it.

"Here, fill this out and return it to me. You can have a seat over there." She pointed across the room to the seats, then turned her back to me and continued her conversation with the others.

I sat there and filled out the paperwork to the best of my recollection. It had questions like the missing person's name, age, last time seen, where were they missing from, were there any identifiable body scars or markings, etc.

When I walked back up to the counter, I had this feeling that I was disturbing these girls. It was as if I was intruding on something private. That's ridiculous I thought because they were at work, not home, and should have acted like professionals not like schoolgirls.

The girl who assisted me earlier, who must have been no more than seventeen, came back to the counter, looked through my paperwork, and then said, "Ok, I will put this in my supervisor's work file. Someone will give you a call."

"Excuse me, I live out of state, do you have any idea how long it will take before someone will contact me?" I asked.

"No ma'am. You pretty much will have to take a number because there are hundreds of files before yours."

"That's not encouraging. Are you telling me that there are hundreds of files already in existence, with only one supervisor working these?" I asked disbelievingly.

"You heard right. We are short staffed around here."

"Well, what do the rest of you do?" I asked.

"Whatever we want," she said as she and the others laughed.

"What is your name?"

"That is my business," she said as she put her hand over her nametag.

"I need to speak to your supervisor."

"Sorry, she's not in today." She smirked.

I was getting heated, but decided not to pursue this. These girls obviously had problems and were looking for a fight. And I wasn't in the mood today.

I gave her a dirty look, turned and walked out. She's not worth it.

Little did I know that after I walked out, she crumpled my papers and threw them into the trash.

The Wait

Months went by. I checked on the status of my paperwork weekly, and was told the same thing, that it wasn't being worked yet. After several months of getting this response and attitude, I decided that I should make another trip to Atlanta. I know they were snowed under with paperwork, but I had a bad feeling about mine.

I went back to Atlanta the following summer where I walked up to the police station's missing person's department again. This time I was greeted with dignity. Before I was even in the door good, a nice-looking black girl greeted me. She was a teenager like the others. She had hazel eyes, shoulder length dark brown hair, creamy brown skin, long eyelashes and she was of slender build.

"May I help you ma'am?" She asked with a wide smile.

I explained to her about my previous visit. She took some basic information from me, and told me to have a seat. She will see what she can find.

After about five minutes, she called me to the counter.

"Sorry, ma'am. Your paperwork was not found. I hate to say this but we had some problems in the past with one girl in particular who destroyed paperwork rather than processing it. She has since been fired. Here take this paperwork, fill it out and I promise you that this won't be discarded. It will get into my supervisor's hands this time."

"Thank you. What is your name young lady?" I inquired.

Just as I asked that, a girl came up from behind her and said, "Hey Cher, did you see Kenny this morning?"

She turned to answer, "No girl. What did Kenny do now?"

Then she remembered that I was on the other side of the counter and said, "I'm sorry ma'am, did you have any more questions?"

"No, I'll just sit over here and fill these out again." I said as I pointed to the nearest chair.

"Ok, but I'm here if you have any questions, okay?"

"Okay, thanks," I said as I walked over to the chair. Such a mannerable young lady I thought.

After I filled out the paperwork again, this time I said a little prayer before handing it to this young lady. She took it, and read over it.

"Interesting," she said.

"Excuse me?"

"This is interesting to me."

"Why? Do you think you know my daughter?" I asked full of hope.

At that moment, when she turned her head to look up at me, from an angle I saw what appeared to be a cherry birthmark on her neck. No, I thought, it couldn't be.

"Young lady, what is your name? I see Cher on your nametag. Is that your real name or a nickname?"

"That's what everyone calls me because of this birthmark on my neck. It's a cherry, and my friends always tease me and call me Cher, or Cherry, as well as some other things. But I think it's interesting because your daughter has the same kind of birthmark that I have. And I too used to live in New York years ago," she added.

My heart started pumping extremely hard.

"What is your real name?"

"It's Marisa."

"Oh, what a pretty name." My hopes faded.

"Yes it is. My mom named me that. Well my adoptive mom that is. I don't mean to be nosey but in reading your paperwork I noticed that your daughter, Bae George was once with a New York family by the name of Martin, and her name at the time was changed to June. My adoptive mother, Margaret, didn't tell me much about my past but when I had questions about being adopted she did tell me that I used to live in New York with a family by the name of Martin, I think. She chose to rename me Marisa because she liked that better than whatever my last name was. I never saw my birth certificate so all I know is what I've been told."

She looked into my eyes and said, "You know, there is something familiar about you. I know I am just meeting you Mrs. Uh…"

"Bailey, Bailey Johnson."

She stepped from behind the counter, gently grabbed me by my arm and said, "Bailey, please sit down. I want to talk to you off the record. I too am looking for a family member, my biological mother. That's why I am working here because I have access to things that the ordinary person wouldn't have access to. As a matter of fact, it's my break time, why don't we walk down to the cafeteria?"

"Ok, sounds good to me." I was certainly intrigued by this young lady.

"Myra, I'll be right back, I'm going on break," she yelled to her coworker as we walked out.

We walked to the cafeteria and sat at one of the tables near the window.

"Bailey, I think we might be on to something here. Let me tell you a little about what I know so we can see if it might help you in your search. The biggest thing that stands out in my mind that I can remember is this lady, who I assume was my mother, was carrying me in a train station and walking down the subway tracks. I know it sounds crazy but for some reason I remember this. I was crying and this woman was very sad. I never saw her again."

After she said this all I could do was cry.

"Oh God! You are my baby, Bae George!"

"Bailey, how could you be so sure?" she asked incredulously as tears started streaming down her cheeks.

"I had a son Brian, who was murdered. To make a long story short I became depressed and flipped out. One of the stupid things that I did, unbeknownst to myself in that frame of mind, was to think about ending our lives so that we could be with Brian and with other loved ones. At that moment my mind told me to walk down some train tracks in Manhattan. Needless to say, the state took you away from me, and adopted you out, and put me in an insane asylum far away from you."

"When I got myself together years later, I started looking for you. And now it looks like I finally found my Bae George!" I exclaimed as

I stood up and gave her hugs and kisses. She was tall and slender and I didn't have far to bend to kiss her. We were almost the same height.

"Could it be true? Could you really be my mother?" she asked.

"There is only one way to truly find out. We could have a DNA test. Oh God, I just know in my heart that you are my baby. I can't wait to find out about all those years that I missed with you."

The Test

Because Marisa worked at the police station, her contacts were able to give us details on how to have a DNA test taken. Then we went to the DNA testing department, signed papers, got swabbed, and were told the results would be available in about two weeks. We didn't have any money but her connection there told me he would bill me. That was good because I never walk around with a lot on me anyway.

My time in Atlanta was up, and it was going to be hard to leave Marisa behind.

"Marisa, we have to keep in touch especially if these results prove that we are mother and daughter. Here's my number and address. What's yours? Oh, wait a minute, do you think your parents would mind?"

"I don't live with them. I um, kind of left home because of circumstances. I am staying in like a shelter home with others my age. I'm kind of emancipated. So I don't run anything by them. Besides, I'm almost eighteen. Here's my information. Please promise me that you will not drop off the face of the earth like you did in the past. I know that you couldn't help that but can you promise me that you won't disappear this time?" Marisa asked.

"I promise."

We hugged and kissed and now it was time for me to make my way back to Jacksonville. It was hard to let go. What if she changed her mind and I never saw her again?

The Wait for the Results

During the weeks that we had to wait for the DNA test results, Marisa and I bonded over the phone. My phone bill was high, but whether or not she turned out to be my daughter, this whole thing was something positive that I needed in my life. And she probably needed this in hers too. I thought I was going to die waiting for the results.

I couldn't eat, I couldn't sleep and I couldn't concentrate at work. I finally received the call that I was waiting for from Marisa.

"Bailey! It's me Marisa!" she exclaimed. She was so excited, I could envision her jumping up and down.

"Of course it's you Marisa, are the results in?"

"Yes! You gotta take time off work to come up here tomorrow. The sooner we find out the better. I just know in my heart that you're my biological mother. And I've been praying that it is so," Marisa said.

"I'll call in a day off tomorrow and take the next bus up. I'll call you from the bus stop here in Jacksonville so that you'll know what time to expect me."

"Ok good, I'll be waiting for you outside the police station," Marisa said.

I paused and said, "Marisa."

"Yes Bailey?"

"Whether this DNA test comes back positive or not, I want you to know that you will always be my daughter. And we will always keep in touch as we continue our search for our biological mother and daughter, okay?"

"Okay. I'll see you tomorrow, mom."

"You are too sweet, I'll see you tomorrow, Bae George."

The DNA Test Results

Marisa was eagerly waiting outside the police station when I walked up. When she saw me, she ran up to me and grabbed my hand.

"It's good to see you again Bailey. Come on," she said as she hurried me into the building.

We walked up to the third floor where the DNA test department was located.

We signed in and sat down. About two minutes later, we were sitting in Mr. Adams' office while he read the test results to us.

"Bailey, Marisa, the DNA test results prove ninety nine point nine percent without a doubt that you two are biological mother and daughter."

We both jumped up screaming, embracing and crying. I showered her cheeks with precious lost kisses.

"Oh God! Yes! I got my baby back! Bae George, honey I love you so much. I mean Marisa. We have so much to catch up on. I'm going to hold you and never let you go."

"Oh Bailey, you're my mom, I can't believe it! Isn't it something how we found each other after all these years? And by accident at that!"

"Well, I am happy to have delivered good news. You two have a lot of catching up to do. Do you want to use my office?" Mr. Adams asked.

"No, that's ok. Mr. Adams we thank you so much," I said as I shook his hand.

Bae George and I walked out hand in hand. We're truly happy. We will *never* come down from this high.

The Miracle

What great news to receive on such a beautiful summer day. To find my baby again after all these years is truly a miracle.

Bae George took the rest of the day off and we went to her group home to get reacquainted with each other. In the group home, she shared a room with two other girls. One of them was home when we came into the room, but left soon after. She probably had a feeling that we needed some privacy. After she left we sat down on Bae George's bed.

"Bae, I mean Marisa, please understand it's gonna be hard to call you that. I still see you as my little Bae George. You were such a pretty little girl and now look at you. You're even more beautiful as a young lady. And you look just like your father. You have his hazel eyes, his smile and even some of his mannerisms."

"Bailey, please tell me about my life with you," Bae George said.

"I will baby, but first I have to catch up on all those years that I missed out on. I have so many questions."

She looked into my eyes and started.

"As far back as I can remember, I lived with the Martins for a short period of time, or at least that's what I was told. They treated me well from what I can remember. Mother, as I called her, treated me like I was a Barbie doll or some prized possession. I remember wearing cute frilly dresses. I was always clean, and if I got a spot on my clothes, she would make me change outfits. My room was filled with what seemed like every doll from the store including expensive porcelain dolls. I had a canopy bed in my room with all the trimmings. Pink was her favorite color, so everything was pink. I had pink sheets, pink curtains, pink dresses, hats and bows. Needless to say, pink is not one of my favorite colors now. I'm sure she meant well. Mother wasn't able to have any kids of her own, and she told me that I was her little gift from God."

"You *are* truly a gift. My gift," I added. My eyes started tearing up just thinking about the things I missed out on.

"I do have to say that I had a lot of fun with her. She took me everywhere. Bought me everything, threw parties for me. All of that in the short period of time that I lived with them."

"What about Mr. Martin? Do you remember anything about him?" I asked.

"Not much because I didn't see him very often. Mother used to fuss at him because he would get home from work too late to tuck me into bed."

"Unfortunately a lot of men are like that. They get home too late to tuck the kid in then they have the nerve to want to wake the kid so that they can play with them. Your dad, George, was not like that though. He died before you were born but he was there for your brother, Brian."

"Tell me about my brother."

"I'll tell you more about him in a few, but I want to finish hearing about your life."

"I was sad when they died. They were the only family I had. Mother killed father then committed suicide, you know."

"I know. How did you feel about seeing her kill herself?"

"I was scared and confused. I felt horrible, and even though I was so young, I was perceptive enough to know that what she did was wrong. And when she put the gun up to her head, I knew she was gonna die and there was nothing that I could do to stop her. So I ran to the phone to dial '0' for the operator. I was crying so hard that I don't think they could understand what I was saying and on top of that I didn't even know my address. Then Isabel came home from the store and found them."

"She ran through the house frantically looking for me. When she found me, she took the phone from me and talked to the operator. The rest is a blur."

"The state put me with Margaret and John Deets immediately. And they eventually adopted me and moved to Georgia. She had a daughter from a previous relationship, Kathy and she and John adopted two boys, Brandon and Gene."

"How did they treat you?" I asked anxiously.

"I guess I should not complain and be thankful that someone wanted me. But living with them was rough."

"In what way?"

"Are you sure you want to hear about this?" Bae George asked as she nervously shifted on the bed.

"Only if you feel up to telling me."

"I do."

We continued talking for hours. At one point during lunchtime, one of the girls kindly interrupted us to give us some sandwiches and sodas.

My jaw dropped as she recounted growing up in Margaret and John's household.

Margaret and John's Home

"From the beginning they treated me as the odd one out. I was the only black person in the family. My brothers were Korean. Well now that I think about it, they weren't treated so hot either. Which made me wonder why they adopted us. Years later Kathy told me that Margaret and John received a monthly check for the boys because they had some kind of medical condition. Money could have been a part of their motivation for adopting them. I was six, Kathy was seven, Brandon was nine and Gene was seven."

"Naturally the girls had a room, and the boys had a room across the hall from us. As soon as I arrived, Margaret took my expensive clothes away from me and put them in Kathy's closet. Kathy was rough on my things and after a while they didn't have the crispness they once had. She also destroyed all my dolls. I don't think she was used to having nice things like that. And Margaret never tried to teach her how to take care of things."

"We all attended the same school. We had to walk straight there and straight back everyday. We had chores waiting for us when we got home. We weren't allowed to go outside until after our homework was done and all the chores were finished. But we had so many chores that most of the time we didn't get to go outside."

"John was a perfectionist and everything had to be in place all the time. When he came home from work if anything was out of place, we were the ones who suffered. Margaret was a slob who sat around the house all day doing nothing. I think she couldn't wait for us to get home so we could do the things that she should have been doing all day long. She probably just sat on the couch smoking her cigarettes while she watched soap operas and drank her beer."

"They were both abusive. They called us mean names sometimes. But we banded together which helped us deal with it. Kathy was treated like gold, but she didn't like the way we were being treated. She always stuck up for us, but was beat down for it."

I tried hard to hold back the tears. No one wants to hear about their child or anybody for that matter going through abuse of any kind.

She continued, "I think both of them were alcoholics because they always sat around and got drunk and obnoxious. Then they would target one of us to pick on. When they were acting this way, that's when most of the abuse happened."

"Oh my God! What kind of abuse?"

"Both verbal and physical. We put up with it for years because we were too afraid to say anything. We figured that either nobody would believe us and we would suffer more, or we'd be taken away and put in a worse situation."

"That's horrible! I am so sorry that you had to go through this. I had no idea. How did you end up here? And where are the others?"

"I just couldn't take it anymore. John got so drunk one holiday that he passed out on the couch. Later that night he came to our room and tried to have his way with Kathy! I was asleep but her muffled screams and her thrashing about on the bed woke me up. After I fully woke up and adjusted my eyes to the darkness, I, well, you can imagine what I saw. So I hopped up and jumped on his back. He knocked me to the floor then Kathy rebounded and jumped on him."

"Oh my goodness. This is too much!"

She had tears in her eyes as she continued, "While we were wrestling with him, Margaret came into the room and stopped the fight. Kathy and I were a little bruised but for the most part we were okay. But Kathy's bruises were more noticeable because of her pale skin color. Without knowing the full story, and without caring to hear it, Margaret took John's side when he said that Kathy enticed him. I was sixteen at the time and was just about as tall as Margaret. I had enough so I jumped into her face to argue with her. I wanted to punch her but had too much respect for my elders. That wimp John left the room and let

Margaret deal with the situation. I told her I had enough of the abuse and this last incident was it! I refused to continue living like this, with her turning a blind eye to his actions. I was so disgusted that I made a beeline for the phone downstairs and dialed the police. While I was waiting for someone to pick up on the other line, Margaret was right there beside me trying to grab the phone out of my hands. As we were struggling, I heard someone pick up so I started yelling into the phone. Margaret was stronger than I was and managed to push me away from the phone and yank the cord away from the wall. She chased me back to my room where I managed to lock the door before she got to it. I felt sorry for Kathy. I tried to talk her into filing a police report but she said she loved her parents and didn't want them to go to jail. She blamed the alcohol, which was a major part of it in my opinion, but I told her they both needed help but didn't realize it. So things can't get better until they realize this and attempt to do something about this problem."

"To make a very long story short, the police traced our number and came by to check out the situation and make a report. Kathy didn't speak up so not much came out of it. More incidents followed which caused the state to forcibly remove us from our home. The boys are happily living in Alpharetta with a foster family. Kathy is across town at a different home. They are more equipped to help her deal with her trauma. She is in therapy because of the abuse she suffered from John. Kathy and I call each other practically every week, and we conference the boys in at least once a month. I sure miss them. We all used to be so close because we only had each other to depend on."

"I don't know what happened to Margaret and John. Last I heard, they moved or ran away before John was scheduled to appear in court for the abuse charges. Their disappearance has hindered Kathy's recovery. That is so sad. She has no closure. I don't understand what kind of parents these are that could do something like this then disappear while Kathy is left to deal with this all alone."

"That is so sad. We will have to pray that she survives and makes it through this. If you can, please make sure that you continue to keep in touch with her. She needs you and the boys. You are her family. Marisa, John didn't do anything inappropriate to you did he?" I cautiously inquired.

She was such a beautiful young lady now. She looked so cute in the yellow jumpsuit that she changed into about an hour earlier. Tall and lean just like how I used to be.

"No Bailey. But it wasn't from a lack of trying. I always tried to make sure that I wasn't alone in the house with him. It took a lot of effort because every chance that Margaret had, she was out the door and we were at John's mercy. One night while Margaret was out, John came into the room. I was in a deep sleep and didn't hear anything. Kathy later told the police that John, who is a big two hundred forty pound man, came into the room and grabbed her out of the bed with his hand over her mouth. He caught her by surprise so she didn't even have a chance. None of us heard a sound. She managed to run away before something happened and someone saw her running down the street and stopped to help her. They took her to the police station, and the rest is history."

"I feel for her, but I am glad that you are all right. He needs to be locked away for what he did."

"And what made this whole thing even worse was the fact that Margaret took his side. How can a mother do that to her child? Kathy didn't deserve any of that. That's the gist of my life. I'm a survivor. I try to keep negative or sad thoughts about my life out of my mind so that I can keep moving on. Can you now tell me about my father and brother?" she asked anxiously.

"Yep but first I have to find somewhere to stay for the night. It's getting late," I said as I looked at my watch.

"There's a hotel down the block. From what I understand their rates are pretty reasonable. Come on, I'll take you there."

We walked down the street to the Sleep Inn Hotel where I was able to secure a room for the night. On our way back to the shelter, we grabbed some take out food and some sodas from the Pizza Palace.

Trip Back to Florida

We went back to Bae George's room where I told her all about her grandmother, her brother and her father. I also told her about Deja and Miles. She told me that she vaguely remembered them and Brian. She was so young at the time.

"Brian was so crazy about you. And if your father had lived, he would have been crazy about you too."

"That's nice to know. I am so sorry that I will never get to know them, but I am thankful to God that I have you again. Now that we are together again, what's next?" Bae George inquired.

"I don't know. What do you think you want?"

"I want to get to know you, Bailey. You're my flesh and blood and it feels so good to know that. For a while there I thought I had no biological family anywhere. Don't get me wrong, I love Kathy, Brandon and Gene. But it is so cool to meet someone who has my same blood running through their veins. And when I look at you, I see some of myself in you. I'll be eighteen in a couple of weeks, and then I will be free to move out of this home. Would it be presumptuous of me to ask if I could move in with you?" she asked while looking up at me with a bright smile on her face.

I got up off the bed, and pulled her over to me. I hugged her dearly and said, "I would be more than happy to have you live with me. I only have a one bedroom apartment right now, so would you mind sleeping on the couch until I can get a sleeper couch for you? Or would you prefer to sleep in the bed and I'll take the couch?"

"Thanks for the offer but I don't care where I sleep. The couch is fine. I just want to be with you. I want to find out what it feels like to be with my biological mother."

"And you will. Marisa you have no idea how much I missed you. I thought about you everyday. And not one day went by without me praying to God for you." I started crying because I thought of all the things I went through all the while worrying about and missing Bae George.

"Don't cry Bailey. We both survived the past and now we are back together again. We should just go forward now and concentrate on our future together, right?" she asked with a smile as she took a tissue to wipe my tears.

I put a hand up to stroke one of her precious cheeks, "Yes you're right. We need to move forward. You are so perceptive for your age. You remind me so much of your brother. I wish I had a picture to show you. I used to have picture albums but I don't know what happened to my things after they put me away in the asylum. Wait a minute I just thought of something, I'll try to get in contact with an old friend from back home, Janice. Maybe she knows what happened to my things. I don't even know if she still lives in Red Hook but it's worth a shot. I don't know why I didn't think about this before. She might even know what happened to Deja and Miles."

"Bailey since I won't be moving for a couple of weeks, this will give me a chance to meet with Kathy and the boys to clue them in on what is going on in my life. I have to check with Kathy's therapist first though because she might take this hard. After all she had a mother, who didn't love her and abandoned her. And here I come with my excitement after finding my real mother, a mother who always loved and wanted me. I don't want to push her deeper into her despair. I love her too much. The boys will be happy for me. And I will promise all of them that I will keep in touch. Maybe one day they could even come to Jacksonville to visit, right?"

"Oh course. My home is your home, and don't you ever forget that, okay Marisa?"

"Ok Bailey," Bae George said.

The next day, it was time for me to get back on the bus to head home to Jacksonville. Bae George had some unfinished business to take care of before making the trip to Florida. Once again, it was hard to leave her especially now after all of this.

"Marisa, you promise to keep in touch?"

"Of course Bailey, and we *will* be together again permanently in a couple of weeks, right?" Bae George said.

"Most definitely." I said as I hugged her.

When I went back to work, I was beaming all day. I was so happy that I had to share my story with everyone! Even with the people who I didn't like.

One of my colleagues, Shirley, was so excited for me that she went out of her way to help me tell the world.

One afternoon she told me, "Bailey, I have a cousin who is a newscaster at 'Eyes on the City News' on channel 8. I told her your story about finding your daughter again after all these years and she wants to interview you and your daughter live! Isn't that exciting? I knew you wouldn't mind so I gave her your number here at work. She'll be contacting you soon. You're welcome."

I wanted to choke her. She always goes out of her way to get into other people's business. Oh well, no sense crying over spilled milk. I looked at her and thanked her for being so caring. That's just great I thought. What if Bae didn't want all of this publicity? What about the asylum? Nah, that was a long time ago. I'm sure that they wrote me off years ago. They probably thought that I died since I was never found, if they indeed had attempted to look for me.

After I thought about it more, I tried to look at it in a positive light. I figured maybe our story could help someone else with their search. And I also thought that maybe this could help me find Deja after all these years…

The Move

While I waited for the weeks to go by, I had a chance to reflect on everything. It was so overwhelming to me. I could only imagine how overwhelming it must have been for Bae George.

I had a chance to give my apartment a deep cleaning. I even looked around for an apartment in a better neighborhood. One day we'll move to a better neighborhood. I don't care if it means living in an apartment or in a house. The latter is my dream though. I always wanted a house for my family.

Bae George arrived in sunny Jacksonville on Amtrak weeks later. All that she had to her name was two large suitcases and a small box that she had previously sent to me via the United Parcel service.

When the train stopped, I saw her eagerly looking through the window for me. And when she saw me she gave me the biggest smile that I've ever seen in my life. She couldn't wait to get off of the train.

"Bailey!" She exclaimed as she waved and ran over to hug me.

"Oh Bae. I mean Marisa, I love you so much. I'm sorry if I am feeling so emotional right now." I said with tears in my eyes.

"I love you too Bailey. Come on! Don't get emotional now! Let's get my stuff and get out of here. I'm so ready to get my life started with you." She said as she grabbed my hand and led me over to the luggage.

Bae George adjusted well at my place. One day while we were relaxing on the couch, she turned to me and said, "Bailey, I've been thinking about my future. I think that I want to go to college to become a doctor."

"A doctor? That's a good profession. What kind of doctor?"

"I don't know yet. I just know that I like people and want to help them."

"Well, I'm sure that you will make a good doctor period," I said.

"Yes, thank you. I will take that compliment." She said with a smile as she closed her eyes as if to daydream about it.

Her grades were so good that she got a scholarship to one of the local Universities. She has dreams of owning her own practice. She decided that she wanted to become a Family Practice doctor to help the less fortunate. She also worked a part time job at one of the downtown banks after her morning classes.

It took months of saving but we managed to accumulate enough money to get a used car. In between all of the things that Bae George did with her time, she also managed to take driving lessons. She was serious and determined about these lessons that she passed her driving test on the first attempt. I noticed that when she put her mind to do something, there was no turning back. This car was a godsend because she no longer had to take several buses out to the University and several buses back to get to her job on time. I only had to take one bus each way to work and our work hours were different so I didn't need to use the car.

This car also made shopping a lot easier. I didn't have to take several buses out to Regency Mall anymore. Bae George and I liked going window-shopping on the weekends. We also talked a lot about the kind of house we'll buy one day. She had no plans to ever leave me. But realistically I knew that one day the time would come for her to go on with her life without me. She is so sweet and loving that I know one day the right guy will come out of nowhere and scoop her up. She is so pretty and has such a great personality that she gets offers to go out all the time. But she always declines because she wants to be with me and claims she is not interested in dating right now. She prefers to concentrate on college and on spending the rest of her time with me. Sometimes we just relax together on the couch and quietly watch television. Or she'll come in my room while I am reading and lay across the bed to study for a test. It's like she never ever wants to be out of my sight. It's a nice feeling. It's like she is my baby again, but yet in a grown up way.

Thank you God, I am so blessed to have her back in my life again. I can't thank you enough.

Bae George welcomed the interview. On the day of the interview, she was happy and bubbly. Things went so well that our story ended up on the World News Tonight broadcast. We received good responses from all over the world. But sadly no response was received from Deja.

Reconnection

A couple of weeks after the newscast I received an unexpected phone call at work.

"Hello, is this Ms. Bailey Branch? The woman who was on the news because she found her daughter who was taken away from her years ago? I didn't personally see the story but friends told me about it. I think that you might be the same Bailey Branch I knew growing up years ago."

I started sweating profusely and reached for a handkerchief to wipe my face.

"Yes I'm Bailey Branch, who's speaking please?" I inquired. This better not be a prank call, I thought to myself.

"This is Miles. Ms. Bailey do you remember me?"

I almost fainted.

"Miles? Is it really you? Oh my God!" I screamed.

Everyone in the office turned around to look at me. Shirley ran over to make sure that I was all right. But I knew that there was another motive there too. She is so nosy.

"Yes Ms. Bailey, it's really me. I sure missed you." "Where, where is Deja? And where are you guys living now? Is she okay? Are you calling me from Jacksonville?"

"Yes, everything is okay. I saw the newscast, and that's how I found you. I hope you don't mind me calling you at work."

"Of course not Miles."

"We're now living in Clearwater Beach Florida. Can we meet up with you this weekend?"

"Yes, here wait a minute, give me your number and address. I don't want to lose you and Deja again."

I grabbed a piece of paper and scribbled down the information. Then I gave him my home number and address.

"I'll have to find out how to get there. How far away is Clearwater Beach from here?"

"It's about four to four and a half hours. I'll make sure that you have directions. You'll have to take 95 South to I-4 West. I'll call you again later this week to give you exact directions to the house. Mom would come up there but at this time she is not in a position to do so. She hopes that you don't mind driving down, you can stay here for the weekend, okay?" Miles said.

"Okay, no problem. We'll come down early Saturday morning. Please tell Deja that I can't wait to see her again. And Miles, thank you so much for contacting me."

"Ms. Bailey, I am so glad that we found you too. See you soon."

"Okay, bye."

"Bye."

After I hung up the phone, I couldn't help but to scream again. I am sure I startled everyone. But given the situation I am sure that they would understand. And if not, I don't care! I found my Deja again! I can't wait to see her.

I had to take a break and walk outside the building. I once again thanked God for everything. And now this is the piece de resistance. To finally find Bae George again, and now Deja and Miles. What more could I ask for?

After Bae George arrived home from work, I told her about my day. She was excited.

"Do you mind driving me?"

"No I don't mind. Can I stay too?"

"Most definitely."

After we ate a quick dinner, I took a long shower and pondered the thought of seeing Deja again. I hope things went well for her all these years. Judging by the address Miles gave me, it looks like she is doing extremely well. She's on the beach. There's nothing but ritzy houses on that section of Clearwater Beach. I am so proud of her.

Days later Miles called and gave me directions. Bae George and I woke up early on Saturday morning. The clock was set for six o'clock. We had a small breakfast and then I took my shower. Bae George had already taken hers before she ate breakfast.

After I dried myself off, I put on a new pair of Lee jeans and a black silk blouse. I love the way this blouse feels against my skin. Then I slipped on a black pair of two-inch pumps.

I noticed Bae George was wearing the same colors. The only difference was that she wore a black tee shirt and black sneakers with her jeans. Regardless of what she wears, she is a natural beauty. No wonder the guys are falling all over her. She still has that creamy glow to her caramel colored skin. The short shiny brown hair that she once had now cascades in ringlets around her shoulders. She doesn't have one blemish on her smooth pretty face.

"Bailey, you ready to go?"

"Yes."

"I'm so excited. Are you going to be okay after not seeing her all these years?"

"I'll be okay. Thanks for coming with me."

"Anytime."

It took us over four hours to find her house. We stopped at a rest area once to use the bathroom. When we arrived in Clearwater Florida, we had to drive across Causeway Boulevard. It was hard to concentrate on the road because the water on both sides of the road was sparkling from the sunrays that were beaming down upon it. She did indeed live on Clearwater beach, off of Mandalay Avenue in a nice house. Her house is a two-story lime green beachfront home with an attached two-car garage. When we pulled into the driveway, Miles came outside and opened my door for me.

"Hi Ms. Bailey."

"Miles, look at how you've grown! You are very handsome!" I exclaimed as I reached up to hug him.

He must have been about six foot three, and one hundred ninety pounds of muscles. I could tell he was built. I would have never imagined that this scrawny kid would have turned out to look like this. His short-cropped haircut really added to his good-looking features.

His chestnut colored face was unblemished and there was a hint of a mustache.

"Thank you Ms. Bailey. It's been a while. I sure missed you and you know…"

"I know."

He hugged me again and said, "I'm so sorry about what happened to Brian. I miss him so much."

"I know so do I."

"I felt bad for years because I never had a chance to tell you that."

"That's all right." At that moment Bae George walked around the car to my side.

"Hi! I'm Marisa. But you know me as Bae George." Bae George said as she reached up to hug Miles.

After the hug, he stood back, looked her up and down and said respectfully, "Bae George, you have really grown up. You are so beautiful. When I saw you last, you were a little knucklehead girl. And your brother and I were your permanent babysitters," he said with a chuckle.

Then he added, "Why did you change your name to Marisa? Which by the way is a pretty name too."

"Come on," she said as she put her arm in his and led him towards the house.

"I'll tell you all about it. But right now, Bailey is dying to see your mom again."

He led us into the spacious well kept home, and called for Deja.

"Mom, Ms. Bailey and Bae George are here!"

We were standing in the richly marbled foyer when Deja appeared at the top of the stairs. We stood in awe as we watched her make her grand entrance down the stairs to the foyer. She was lovely in a short gorgeous blue velvet mini skirt set with matching blue velvet leather pumps.

"Bay, is it really you?" she said when she reached the last step.

"Oh Deja! I missed you so much!" I said as I reached over and hugged her.

"Oh my God! I can't believe we are together again!"

We were both crying so hard, it was difficult to see each other.

"Look at my baby," I said as I pulled Bae George over to Deja.

She gave her a kiss and said, "You have really grown up young lady. You look so much like your dad. You are so beautiful and just look at your pretty curls. And oh Bay, look at her cute little shape. She gets that from you."

"I'm glad because for a minute there I was starting to think that I didn't have anything to do with her good looks. And Deja I have to say that Miles has really grown up well too. He's grown into a very handsome young man. He's quite mannerly too."

"Thanks girl. Come on let's go into the living room."

"Mom, we're going to be in the family room. That way you two can talk in private," Miles said.

"Ok."

We walked into a wonderfully decorated living room. Deja had a rich red Italian leather sofa with a matching loveseat and ottoman. Behind the sofa was a mirror that was encased in red leather that was sewn around the frame. The carpet was black, and the curtains were made of black and red silk. That's Deja for you, she still had outlandish taste. There were matching glass end tables and a glass coffee table. The two lampshades were made of the same black and red silk as the curtains. There were a lot of expensive Lladro porcelain figurines on bookshelves that were made of rich mahogany. This room was very cozy.

I was the first to speak after we melted into the couch.

"Deja, where have you been? I tried to reach you years ago but couldn't find you."

"Girl let me tell you. Where should I start? First of all would you like something to drink? It's gonna be a long day."

"I'll have whatever you're having."

She got up, walked over to the bar and poured both of us a glass of Merlot wine.

"Here you go," she said as she handed me the expensive Waterford crystal wine glass.

"Thanks."

"Ok, let me see. The last time we spoke was that Thanksgiving after we left Red Hook. Right? Or one of those holidays, anyway things initially were going really well for us. We lived in a nice apartment downtown and Miles had a good paying job working for the post office. Little Miles went to a magnet school of the arts. Life was good at that time. But eventually he started cheating on me. I know you were concerned about that since he was still married when he messed with me. But I thought he had changed. That's the main reason why I didn't call you as often as I know I should have. I was too embarrassed. I also found out that he kept delaying our wedding because he was still married to Kim! He did finally divorce her to marry me. Then about six months later, my world started unraveling around me. I blamed myself because I was thinking of leaving Miles around that time, which caused a lot of guilt."

"One night in the early part of the following year, there was a fire at the apartments. This building had about twenty floors, and we lived on the twelfth floor. Little Miles was a couple of floors down from our apartment at a friend's place, Miles was in the apartment sleeping, and I was one floor down at a neighbor's apartment. My neighbor and I were sitting around talking and having a few mixed drinks, when I noticed the smell of smoke. At first I tried to dismiss it as my imagination. Then all of a sudden we heard a loud fire alarm going off in the hallway. We ran out and saw smoke everywhere. She yelled to run out the building, and proceeded to do so. I didn't run out the building, instead I ran down the steps to the apartment where little Miles was playing cards with his friend, but by the time I got there they were gone. So then I ran upstairs to wake up big Miles. It was hard to breathe and see because thick smoke filled the air, and fire was coming through the walls and the doors. When I reached what I thought was my apartment, from what I was later told, I went to open the door and my hands got burned from the door knob. Then the door exploded in my face causing me to fall back and crack my head against the hallway wall."

"Oh my God," I said as I held my hand up to my mouth. I was horrified.

"I was in a coma for a couple of weeks and when I woke up out of it I was told that my in laws had taken care of little Miles and sadly Big Miles had perished in the fire."

"Oh Deja, I am so sorry about your loss. I had no idea. I know that was hard for you."

"I totally lost it. I was glad Miles was okay. He's my baby. But to find out about the love of my life dying! That was too much. And to add insult to injury I had third-degree burns on my face and hands and the apartment owners, Grant & Sons didn't want to take responsibility for the fire. The fire department ruled it as an electrical fire. Some of the wiring was frayed and they don't know how this building even passed inspection."

"I retained an attorney and sued Grant & Sons. We ended up settling out of court. One condition of the settlement stated that they were to pay my hospital bill and for all of my subsequent visits for skin grafting and whatever else was necessary to get my skin healthy again. They also paid for Miles' funeral. And because I was in a coma, his parents handled everything for me. I was able to repay them for the out of pocket expenses that they paid upfront for the funeral. Grant & Sons were also ordered to pay for any necessary psychiatric visits that we needed to help us deal with this tragedy. And of course I received a large lump sum of money in addition to those stipulations."

I lifted up one of her hands and smoothed a finger over her skin. These must have been some really nasty burns because I could see where some of the skin had been grafted on.

"See, my other one is like that too," Deja said as she lifted the other one and showed me some of the grafting.

"Did it hurt?"

"The burns hurt more so than the grafting. The doctors told me that one day I will be back to normal. And look at this scar on my nose," she said as she moved some of her long cornrow braids out of her face for me to see.

"What scar? I don't see any."

"Ah ha! That's 'cause there aren't any," she said with a smile. Then continued, "They grafted skin there so perfectly that I can't even tell. That's how I know that they will be able to do the same to my hands."

"Oh Deja, I am so sorry you had to go through all of that."

"I know but some good did come out of it."

"What?"

"It made me stronger. At first I was depressed and kept to myself a lot. I didn't go out, and I didn't socialize or answer the phone. Poor Miles used to beg me to go out like I used to but I just couldn't bring myself to have any fun. How could I possibly enjoy life knowing that my Miles was dead, and I could have done something to avoid it?"

"Deja, you know it wasn't your fault."

"At the time I didn't realize it but I know now. My therapist helped me sort through that. With his help I slowly started coming out of my depression. I learned to love and appreciate life again. This was good for Miles too because he now had his mother back. That's one strong young man. During that time he took care of a lot of things that I should have, and never once complained. He learned how to budget money for food shopping, he learned how to keep house and how to cook. I don't know how I could have made it without him. He's a blessing. I was also depressed because I lost touch with you. And I couldn't understand how. I tried contacting you before the fire and when I couldn't reach you, I called Janice. She told me about Brian. And Bay, I am dearly sorry," she said as she reached over and patted my hands.

Then she continued, "I should have told you this from the jump. But stupid me, I just had to go on about myself."

"Don't be silly! I told you to talk about yourself. I did have a hard time dealing with Brian's murder, and to this day I don't know if they caught those murderers. Even though it took years I have since let it go by forgiving them in my heart otherwise I wouldn't have been able to go on with life. I would have been stuck in the past. It's okay, Deja, go on with what you was saying."

"Janice and I cried as we talked about Brian. I asked her if she knew what had happened to you. She told me that months after his death, you and Bae George had disappeared. And the landlord came to her one day asking if she knew where you had gone. He told her that he was going to put your apartment up for rent if the rent was not paid within that week. And after that he was going to sell your furniture because he didn't have the money to put it in storage. Janice managed to persuade him to let her box up your personal items and hold on to them for you."

"Really? Oh my God! I don't care about the furniture, but I am so glad that she kept my stuff. How sweet is that? Is she still living in Red Hook after all these years?"

"As far as I know. I thought about getting your things back when I first spoke with her, but I am glad that I didn't because of the fire. But, I did get them a couple of years ago. Because I knew in my heart that we would be together again."

"Deja, I love you. Thank you so much. And I have to thank Janice too. You still have her number, right? God has been so good to us. He helped us survive our tragedies. There must be a reason why we are still alive."

"Yep, and one of those reasons is so that we can party! We got to celebrate finding each other again. Just think after all these years, we're together again!"

"Yes we are. I love you sis."

"Bay tell me about what you went through after Brian's death. Well, only if you feel up to talking about it. I know that must be a sensitive subject."

"I'm okay now. But back then I was a wreck. I felt so lonely because I lost Brian, and I didn't have my husband or my mom, or you for that matter. And I'm sure poor Bae George must have been confused by my behavior."

We talked for hours as I told Deja about the details of our years apart. Including how I ended up in Jacksonville and the details about Bae George's life with her adoptive parents.

"It's gonna be strange calling her Marisa."

"It is strange, but you know, she will always be Bae George to me. So I don't care if I have to call her Marisa or Frannie or Dawnie or whatever, as long as we are together, it doesn't matter."

"True that!" Deja cried.

"Oh look at the time," I said as I looked at my watch. "Deja, you gotta show me your home. So far I have been impressed with what I have seen."

"There's no hurry 'cause you're staying the weekend, right?"

"Yep."

"Let's finish our drinks then."

After about twenty minutes Deja put her glass down and said, "Come on," as she walked towards the stairs.

This was a two-story home. We walked upstairs where she showed me five lavishly decorated bedrooms with adjacent full sized bathrooms.

All of the bathrooms were equipped with an enormous garden tub and a walk in shower that was large enough for several people.

Miles' room was decorated with a masculine theme. He had a king sized bed and the colors in the comforter were a mixture of deep blues and greens. I could tell that he had a hand in the decorating. His room was at the opposite end of the hall from Deja's room.

"This is really nice."

"Yes, he put a lot of thought into the decorations. Now he's ready to be out on his own so he just found a nice apartment about ten miles away. He'll be moving and taking all of his stuff."

"That's right! He's a grown man now and needs to spread his wings. At least he won't be too far from you," I said.

"That's true girl. He has a good job and has never asked me for anything. And he's pretty stable so I know that he will be okay on his own," Deja said.

We then walked into Deja's room.

Deja's room was off the chain. Anything that you could imagine having in a room for comfort was in her room. She had a king sized cherry wood framed bed with an expensive tri-color silk comforter, with a matching bed skirt. There were several different sized pillows on the bed. There were two nightstands and two matching expensive cherry wood armoires. Just about everything was accessed by remote control. She had a remote control to access the television, the lights, and the curtains. And the list goes on. On the other side of the curtains, was a window that was the full length and width of a wall, and one could peer through it to look at the ocean. In the middle of the window was a set of French doors that easily accessed the balcony.

In her bathroom around the garden tub, there were all sorts of expensive scented candles, and bubble bath bottles. The garden tub had small blocked glass windows above it so that no one could see in from the outside. But the chances of that was slim because the windows were on the second floor and the only thing that was on the other side was the beach and the ocean.

"Man if I lived like this, I wouldn't ever have any stress. I love looking at the waves on the ocean. I bet it's really beautiful at night when the moon is out and all that you can hear is the splashing of the waves," I said.

"Yes it is. I often keep one of my French doors open so that I can hear it and feel the breeze," Deja said.

The guest rooms were cozy as well. They too were richly decorated. These were the type of rooms that a guest would want to live in forever.

There was also a separate washer and dryer room and a guest bathroom downstairs. Deja also had a library that had several bookcases with too many books to count. The large eat in kitchen had a large island in the center of the room. There was also a grand room that housed a large table with seating for six, an expensive chandelier and a china cabinet. I peeked inside the china cabinet and I could tell that she had only the finest china.

There were stairs leading from Deja's balcony directly down to the beach. And the beach could also be accessed through the back door downstairs.

I could go on and on. This was truly a dream home and I am glad to know that Deja was richly compensated for everything that she and Miles went through. I know that a lot of times people don't win lawsuits against big rich companies, but she persisted and won!

"Come on, let's take a walk on the beach. Roll up your jeans and hold your shoes so that they don't get ruined," Deja said.

"Okay."

We walked out to the beach. We took our time as we slowly strolled down the beach. I felt the crunching of the white sand beneath my feet.

"Deja I can't come this far and not get my feet wet in the gulf waters. Come on."

"Ok, just don't throw or splash any water on me. I don't want you to mess up my braids or my clothes."

"You are so silly. I know how prissy you are. You have nothing to worry about."

As I walked into the water, I noticed that the gulf water looked blue from a distance but up close it was a deep green color that looked a little diluted. I remembered to put my hair up but realized as the sun was beating down on my neck that I didn't have on any sunscreen. Looking into the water I saw little fish swimming around my feet that looked like little white sharks that were being pushed back and forth in the water by the waves.

When I bent down to pick seashells and rinse them off in the gritty, sandy water, I could feel the sand slipping out from beneath my feet as if the Earth was disappearing.

Since it was the winter of 1995, the weather was obviously not miserably hot, but it was hot enough for some people to rent umbrellas while others laid out on the beach. I guess those were the die hards who were determined to come to Florida on vacation and return home with a tan as evidence.

The more we walked, the fewer people we saw basking in the sun because it was now setting. The people who were parasailing were calling it quits as well as the people who were playing volleyball. There were fewer sailboats and sightseeing ships in the distance, and people who were out taking pictures were now leaving the beach.

Since we have been walking for what seemed like hours, we turned around and started heading back to Deja's house.

The creamy blue sky was gone now and it was getting dark but the moon was shining brightly illuminating our way, and there were some other people still out walking too.

"Bay could you come stay with us? We have more than enough room. I really don't want to chance losing you again. I don't think I could handle that again."

"Deja, you know we can't live with you."

"Why not? Give me one good reason why not?" Deja said with one hand on her hip.

"Well, we couldn't afford the rent."

"The house is paid for, so it would be free room and board. And free food and electricity and water too. You wouldn't have to pay for anything except for the bills that you already have. And if I could talk you into letting me take care of those, you wouldn't have those either, but I know you."

"You're right."

"You have no excuse."

"Well, you know what they say about two women living together. And on top of that, we are friends. I don't want to do anything that could ruin our friendship."

"Come on Bay, think about it. For some women it doesn't work, but we are different. We love each other, we are sisters who have been through so much and we need each other. Come on, give it a try, please? For me? For you? For us? Pretty please?" she said as she stopped walking and leaned her head against mine.

"Ok, let me sleep on it and discuss it with Bae. And I'll let you know in the morning. Is that fair?" I relented.

"Yes! Come on, let's go back to the house and eat dinner. And then we can have some cheesecake and some whip cream and stay up all night and talk again. Just like old times! Last one in is the rotten egg!" she yelled as she ran back ahead of me.

I just stood there and looked up to the sky and prayed to God. Thank you God, for giving me my family back. I owe you so much. You have truly connected all the missing pieces of my life.

"Hey what 'cha doing?" Deja said as she ran back to me breathlessly.

"I was just having a private conversation with God," I said.

Then I cheated and sprinted for the house.

"Hey! Wait for me!" Deja said as she caught up to me.

It was so funny, we ran like we were kids. Then we stopped at the back of her house and hugged each other and laughed so hard until we cried.

We stood facing each other. Deja was the first to say something.

"Bay, I am truly blessed to have you in my life again. Our lives are complete again. We've come full circle. Please promise me that we will always be together, no matter what."

I looked her squarely in the face and responded, "Deja, I promise from this day forward, we *will always* be together. We will never lose each other ever again. I love you with every inch of my heart."

She put a hand over her chest and made a motion as if she was touching her heart, smiled at me then proceeded to walk into her house. I followed closely behind…